# FAIRY LIES

# FAIRY LIES

## E. D. BAKER

**BLOOMSBURY**

NEW YORK   LONDON   NEW DELHI   SYDNEY

First published in the United States of America in February 2012
by Bloomsbury Children's Books
Paperback edition published in August 2013
www.bloomsbury.com

For information about permission to reproduce selections from this book, write to
Permissions, Bloomsbury Children's Books, 1385 Broadway, New York, New York 10018
Bloomsbury books may be purchased for business or promotional use. For information on
bulk purchases please contact Macmillan Corporate and Premium Sales Department at
specialmarkets@macmillan.com

The Library of Congress has cataloged the hardcover edition as follows:
Baker, E. D.
Fairy lies / by E. D. Baker. — 1st U.S. ed.
p.      cm.
Sequel to: Wings.
Summary: Half-fairy Tamisin and her boyfriend, Jak, have been arguing over whether
she should return to the land of the fey when Oberon, king of the fairies, kidnaps
her and Jak must return to that place of fairies, goblins, and sphinxes to rescue her.
ISBN 978-1-59990-550-1 (hardcover)
[1. Fairies—Fiction. 2. Kidnapping—Fiction. 3. Oberon (Legendary character)—Fiction.
4. Titania (Fictitious character: Shakespeare)—Fiction. 5. Animals, Mythical—Fiction.
6. Imaginary creatures—Fiction. 7. Magic—Fiction.] I. Title.
PZ7.B17005Fai 2012        [Fic]—dc23        2011025661

ISBN 978-1-61963-035-2 (paperback)

Book design by DDesigns
Typeset by Westchester Book Composition
Printed and bound in the U.S.A. by Thomson-Shore Inc., Dexter, Michigan
2  4  6  8  10  9  7  5  3  1

*This book is dedicated to Ellie and Kim
for their encouragement and support,
to Victoria for being such a wonderful teacher,
and to my fans for believing in me*

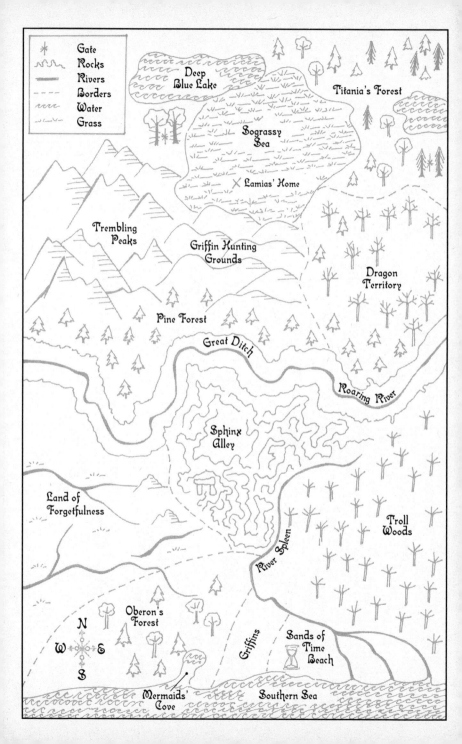

FAIRY
LIES

# Chapter 1

Tamisin had to dance. Although the sky was overcast and the full moon was hidden behind the clouds, the moon still called her to raise her arms, twirl on her toes, and move to music only she could hear. Her long blond hair floated around her, brushing the wisteria blossoms each time she twirled by her parents' back porch. Her bare feet left imprints on the grass as she stepped around the bird-bath in the center of the yard. Her eyes, raised to the concealed moon, didn't seem to notice what was around her but shone as if she had glimpsed something far more wonderful than anything either the human or fey world could offer.

When Tamisin Warner danced, she was as graceful as a woodland creature, her movements as fluid as water rippling over unseen stone. Each step, each gesture, evoked the essence and mystery of the fey world. Anyone who had ever seen her dance could tell that it was as hypnotic for the dancer as it was for the spectator.

That night, Tamisin had been dancing for only a few minutes when the fairies arrived. They came in a cloud of sparkling lights to hover around her, watching silently until her very last gesture. When Tamisin's arms fell to her sides and she took a long, shuddering breath, the fairies fled.

Fairies were nothing new to Tamisin; she had been a child in a human family the first time she felt the urge to dance under a full moon and had seen fairies every month since. Even so, she had been shocked when wings sprouted from her own back and she learned that she might not be as human as she'd always assumed. In fact, no sooner was she whisked off to the fairies' land than she learned that she was adopted and her birth mother was Titania, the queen of the fairies. According to Titania, her birth father was a human named Bottom who had died centuries before. She also learned that the fairies were very strange, so she had found her way home to the human world again. Still, it seemed neither place felt right.

After the first month back in the human world, Tamisin began to feel restless. She started going for short walks around the neighborhood and one day ended up in the woods behind the school, standing in front of the two tall trees that formed a gate to the land of the fey. There were no shimmering lights between the trees, which meant that the gate wasn't open. A few days later Tamisin went for another walk, purposefully heading in a different direction, and ended up in the same place. She tried it again over the weekend and wound up standing in front of the still-closed gate.

Tamisin arrived at school early the next morning to wait by her boyfriend Jak's locker. He was a cat goblin and had visited the land of the fey with her. "What's up?" he said as he walked down the hall. He gave her a quick kiss and added, "You're never here before I am."

"I just wanted to talk," she said, leaning against the next locker as he started his combination.

"Is something wrong?" he asked, frowning.

"Not wrong, exactly. Just odd. You've been busy with basketball practice and, well, I've been really restless lately and have started taking walks. The weird thing is, no matter where I go, I end up in the woods behind the school. There's a gate near that waterfall you took me to last autumn."

Jak's frown deepened. "You've been going to a gate to the land of the fey?"

Tamisin nodded. "Yes, but it's never open. And I'm not *trying* to go there. I just end up standing in front of it somehow."

"Do you want to go back to the land of the fey already?"

"Not really. I'm sure I will someday, but not yet. I hated that so much time passed here while we were there for only a few days. We missed Thanksgiving and Christmas and Petey's birthday. I really wanted to be here for my little brother's birthday party; I was going to put it on for him this year."

"What about Titania?"

"I don't have any burning desire to see her again, if that's what you're asking. She is my birth mother, but I don't think I'll ever feel as close to her as I do to Mom. Janice is the only mother I've ever known. She took care of me whenever I was sick, she read me to sleep when I was little, she taught me how to tie my shoes . . . She's *Mom*, and I guess she always will be. Titania is beautiful and exciting and pretty amazing. But I feel more like she's a really cool aunt I didn't know I had until now. What about you? Do you ever think about visiting your old home?"

"You mean my uncle Targin's cave? All the time," said Jak. "And then I'm grateful that I don't have to. You have no idea how much happier I am here in the human world. I have friends here, and family who care about me. Gammi is the only relative I have who showed me any kindness, and she lives here now. And Bert is like a big brother who would do anything for me. He may be a bear goblin, but I'm closer to him than I ever was to my cousin Nihlo. I still have nightmares where Nihlo is chasing me through the corridors, threatening to lock me outside at night so the lamias will eat me. You can't imagine how scary that was for a little kid. At least here there aren't trolls, or manticores, or other creatures that would want to eat you."

"That's true," said Tamisin.

"I couldn't go back now, anyway," said Jak. "I'm sure all the cat goblins hate me for siding with Titania against my uncle Targin. Given half a chance, they'd probably skin me alive and serve me for dinner."

Tamisin shifted the books she was carrying. "You wouldn't have to see your relatives. The land of the fey is a pretty big place."

"Why would I want to go back? I have everything I need right here. Including you."

Tamisin smiled. She was glad she'd talked to Jak. Just telling someone about it made her feel better. She really didn't want to go back to the land of the fey, at least not for a good long while.

Although she tried to put the gate and the land of the fey out of her mind and stopped going for walks, the desire to visit the gate continued to build inside her. A few weeks later she couldn't stand it any longer and returned to the woods behind the school. There were still no shimmering lights between the trees. Nor were there any the next time she went, or the time after that. She no longer tried to fight the urge to go to the woods, but every time she went, the gate was closed, and she became increasingly frustrated.

"Is something wrong?" Jak asked one day at school after she had snapped at her friend Heather.

"Yes, but you won't want to talk about it," Tamisin told him, slamming her locker door.

"What is it?" he asked. "Did someone do something?"

Tamisin shook her head. "Nothing like that. It's just that . . . I went to the gate yesterday, but it's closed—again!"

"How often have you gone there?"

Tamisin looked away. "At least twice a week for the last two months. But don't worry, it's been closed every time."

"Are you trying to go to the land of the fey?" he said, sounding incredulous.

"Yes . . . No . . . Maybe . . . I don't know what I'm trying to do!" she said. "I guess I just want to see if I *could* go back. If I wanted to, I mean."

"Why didn't you tell me?"

"Because I know how much you don't want to go back!"

"So you'd go without me? Tamisin, do you know how dangerous that would be?"

"Not if I went through the gate behind the school. It goes directly to Titania's forest."

Jak put his hands on her shoulders. "There is no completely safe place in the land of the fey. Promise me you won't go alone."

"I can't promise anything," she said, pulling away.

"It's Titania's kiss. It makes you want to go back to her."

"Then it was a pretty powerful kiss! I can't sleep most nights, and when I do, I dream about the land of the fey. I went flying last week, but the urge to go through the gate kept me flying in circles above it when I saw it was closed again. I can't fly or talk to fairies or dance without wanting to go through the gate even more, so I've stopped flying, and I've yelled at the fairies so often that they come around only when I dance. The one thing I can't do is stop dancing, and believe me, I've tried. I've barricaded my bedroom door with my dresser, and I've tied my ankles to my bed, yet I still find myself outside dancing with my hair a tangled mess and my feet bare and half frozen. I don't know what to do, and it's driving me crazy!"

"I've heard that no one can withstand the compulsion

of the fairy queen's kiss," said Jak. "But I didn't know it was this bad. I guess you don't have any choice about returning to her."

"Well, I'm not going, am I?" said Tamisin. "She kissed me, but she must not really want me there if the gate is always closed. Unless . . . Do you know of any other gate that leads directly to Titania's forest?"

Jak shook his head. "Sorry, I don't."

Tamisin leaned against the locker behind her and closed her eyes. "It's probably just as well. I'd have to tell my family before I left, and I don't know how they'd take it."

Although Tamisin didn't mention the gate to Jak again, she had no intention of quitting. She continued to visit the gate every few days but never did find it open. Then one night Jak invited her to his house for dinner. Knowing how much his grandmother liked mice and raw meat, she wasn't sure she wanted to go. When she arrived, she was relieved to learn that Bert was cooking dinner. He served panfried trout, biscuits with honey, and berries that he'd bought frozen and weren't quite thawed.

"Dinner was delicious," she told the bear goblin as he licked berry juice from his fingers.

"Glad you liked it," he said. "We had fish last night, too. Catfish," he said, grinning at Gammi.

"Odd name for a good fish," said the old cat-goblin woman. "We had it 'cause my cousin Sulie came for a quick visit," she told Tamisin. "The gate between the cat-goblin clan home and our backyard was open, so she stopped by. Didn't stay more than a few hours, which is just as well. For some reason the gates are slow to open but close mighty fast. We had a good visit, though. I liked catching up with all the goings-on back home."

"If she was here for a few hours," said Jak, "I wonder how long she was gone from the other side."

Gammi shook her head. "There's no saying. Time passes differently here and there from one visit to the next. Why, I remember when—"

"Excuse me," Tamisin said, turning to Jak. "Do you mean to say that the gate behind your house was open and you didn't tell me?"

Jak saw the look on her face and his expression turned serious. "I didn't think it mattered. You wouldn't want to go through it anyway. It leads to the center of the cat-goblin clan!"

"Just because you don't want to go that way doesn't mean I can't! I could fly from there to Titania's forest."

"And have a dragon pluck you from the sky? Or a flock of harpies mug you? Or a goblin shoot you down with poison-tipped arrows? Flying can be just as dangerous as walking in the land of the fey. I don't want you going there by yourself, and *I* don't dare go through that gate."

"Or any gate, apparently!" said Tamisin. "You know I want to go back, and you haven't even looked for another way to get there."

"I didn't know it was that important to you," Jak began.

"How can you say that?" Tamisin pushed her chair back and stood. "I told you I was checking the gate every few days to see if it had opened. If it wasn't important to me, do you honestly think I would have kept going back? It's gotten so bad that when I go to the woods and the gate is closed, my heart pounds, my stomach hurts, I break out in a sweat, and I can barely breathe. I'm having anxiety attacks just because that gate is closed, and I'm having them every single time I go there. This isn't like wishing I could go to a party and being disappointed because I can't go. This is like needing to swim to the surface of the water because I'm at the bottom of the pool and running out of air! Thank you for dinner," she told Bert and Gammi. "I hate to eat and run, but I really need to go now."

"Tamisin . . . ," said Jak, but she had already left the room. A moment later she was out the door and hurrying down the sidewalk.

Tamisin was furious. Jak knew exactly how important this was to her. He was the one who had told her about the effect the fairy queen's kiss had on people in the first place! He was afraid to go back, so he didn't want her to go either. Well, forget him! She didn't need him, or Titania either, for that matter. If the fairy queen had wanted her to return to the land of the fey, she would have made sure Tamisin could get back. Tamisin had heard somewhere that fairies were known to be fickle; her mother had probably already changed her mind about having her half-human daughter around.

As days passed, Tamisin's resentment grew. The desire to return to the land of the fey became her constant shadow. Short of living beside the gate and waiting for it to open, there wasn't much she could do, so she did her best to focus on being human.

One day her mother passed by the bathroom while Tamisin was putting on makeup. Tamisin looked up when she realized that her mother was watching her.

"Why are you covering your spreckles?" her human mother asked. "I thought you stopped doing that a while ago. And you're wearing your hair down over your ears. I think it looks so cute pulled back into a ponytail."

Tamisin shrugged. "I'm trying to look more human, and that's really hard with pointed ears like mine, or glittery freckles on my cheeks."

"Is everything all right? Your father and I have noticed that you don't smile as much as you used to, and we hardly ever hear you laugh. You know you can talk to us if something is bothering you."

"Nothing is bothering me," Tamisin said, forcing herself to smile. She loved her parents and didn't want to hurt them; she was sure that hearing how much she wanted to return to the land of the fey would upset them.

That night, Tamisin was on her way to bed when she passed her parents' room and overheard them talking in quiet voices. She couldn't hear much other than her name, but they sounded worried. Although it made her want to run into the room to reassure them, there wasn't anything reassuring about the way she felt, and she really didn't know what to say.

Tamisin continued to visit the gate, her frustration growing each time she saw that it was still closed. She would have had plenty to say to Titania about the kiss, the closed gate, and the confusion that she felt over going to the land of the fey, but with no way to talk to Titania, she turned her anger on Jak.

"Tamisin!" he called down the school corridor one day after she'd spent weeks ignoring his phone calls and avoiding him at school. "We need to talk."

"No, we don't," she said, turning away so she wouldn't have to see the hurt in his eyes that was reflected in the pit of her stomach. She knew she was being unreasonable, but seeing him just made her angrier. Not only had he not told her about the gate but he was half cat goblin, and reminded her all the more of the land of the fey. It was harder to feel human when Jak was around.

A tree frog called from her neighbors' lily pond, sounding like a chick in a henhouse; the noise brought Tamisin fully back to the present. When she saw that she was standing in the yard in her nightgown once again, she shook her head and sighed. Tugging her fingers through the snarls that twirling had whipped into her hair, Tamisin started toward the back door, hoping she had come out that way so the door would be unlocked. (Once, she'd climbed out her bedroom window to dance and had to climb back through in the middle of the night.) She had almost reached the steps to the porch when she sensed movement behind her and glanced back. A human-sized fairy stood in the trees at the edge of the yard. Tamisin gasped. Usually the fairies who watched her were tiny—and harmless.

The fairy stepped out of the shadows and into the light cast by the carriage lamp beside the door, revealing his narrow face; his thin, pointed ears; and the tilt of his bright green eyes. He was taller than most full-sized fairies and wore the subdued browns and greens of a warrior. Sweeping his peaked cap off his head, he bowed in a courtly manner. "I am sorry to startle you, Your Highness. My name is Mountain Ash. You're Princess Tamisin, are you not?" he asked.

"I am," she replied.

"I had heard of the pull fairies feel when you dance, but I did not know how strong it was until I experienced it for myself. I am glad the rumors were true, for it helped me find you. I've come to give you news about your father."

Tamisin frowned. "My birth father died hundreds of years ago."

"Someone has lied to you," said Mountain Ash. "Your father is very much alive. If you come with me, you will see that I'm telling the truth." The fairy held out his hand as if to grasp hers.

Tamisin took a step back. This was too much like the stranger danger they taught little kids about in school. "There's no way I'm going with you," she said. "I have an English final in the morning, and I need to get some sleep."

The fairy warrior sighed and moved toward her. "I had hoped it wouldn't come to this," he said, and raised his hand toward her cheek.

Tamisin slipped out of reach, but before she could take another step, his hand was touching her shoulder, and an instant later, everything began to change. She started to run, but her entire body felt fizzy, as if bubbles were popping inside her. Tiny lights exploded around her; she could see them even after she shut her eyes. When she opened her eyes again, the trees, the house, and the birdbath all seemed to be growing until they towered above her. Soon the grass itself was higher than her head. She cried out when an enormous hand closed around her and squeezed just enough to pick her up. Then she fell into the gaping mouth of a brown sack and was engulfed in darkness and stale air. She landed on her side with a gasp as her breath was forced from her lungs.

"Oberon thinks it's time you met your real father," Mountain Ash's voice boomed as the opening over her head shrank to a tiny circle, then disappeared altogether, cutting her off from light and any hope of fresh air.

Tamisin rolled over and tried to stand, staggering when the bag rose and the bottom curved under her feet.

Small bits of dried leaves crunched beneath her, releasing the scent of mint. She could tell that she was rising by the way she suddenly felt heavier. There was a rushing sound in her ears, and Tamisin passed out.

# Chapter 2

J ak was in his bedroom in the human world, sound asleep on his back, when something touched the tip of his nose. His cat-goblin reflexes woke him with a snort. At first he thought his grandmother might need him, but Gammi slept in the room next to his, and he could hear her snoring through the wall. Opening his eyes, he saw the twinkling lights of two tiny fairies hovering inches above his face. "What do you want?" he grumbled.

Fluttering their wings, the fairies rose in the air until Jak no longer had to look at them cross-eyed. He didn't bother turning on a light; his cat-goblin blood allowed him to see in the dark nearly as well as he could in the daylight.

A moment later two full-sized female fairies were standing on either side of his bed. "We came to tell you what happened," the fairy dressed in green said with a quaver in her voice.

The other fairy gnawed on a lock of her long pink hair the same shade as her flower-petal dress. Spitting the hair out of her mouth, she said, "We know how much you care about the princess. She was wrong to send you away."

"What are you talking about?" Jak turned his head toward the alarm clock on his bedside table. It was 3:41 a.m. He groaned. "Is this your idea of a joke?" he asked. "I'm not discussing my life with you in the middle of the night or any other time. If you think I'm—"

"Quiet, goblin! We came to tell you something important!" snapped the pink-haired fairy.

The other fairy wrung her hands in distress. "Let me tell him, Pansy!"

"It was my idea, Algae," Pansy hissed, "so I should be the one to—"

"Would one of you just tell me!" Jak snapped.

"The princess, Tamisin, has been kidnapped!" blurted Algae.

"What do you mean?" Jak's first thought was that this was a fairy prank.

"Abducted, run off with, taken away, stolen—" Algae began.

"I got that part!" said Jak. Wide awake now, he saw the worried looks on their faces. Jak had met plenty of fairies, and none of them were this good at acting. They had to be telling the truth. He ran his fingers through his hair as he tried to gather his thoughts. "One at a time, tell me exactly what happened. You go first," he told Algae.

"Once upon a time—" Algae began.

"Don't start that far back!" cried Pansy. "We were with

the other fairies who were keeping an eye on the princess," she told Jak. "Ever since the princess came back to this world, some of us have been watching to make sure she's all right. And she was, until tonight."

Algae nodded. "We try to stay out of sight, but we can't help going closer when she dances under a full moon. Tamisin gets annoyed when she sees us, so we leave as soon as we can."

"We don't go far," said Pansy. "So we saw when he came."

"When who came?" Jak demanded.

"Mountain Ash. He's a colonel in Oberon's army," Pansy replied. "He showed up right after the princess danced. They were talking, and then all of a sudden he touched her and she shrank."

"We couldn't stop him!" Algae cried. "Before we knew what he was up to, he had stuffed the princess into a bag, then shrunk himself, and . . ."

"And a whole bunch of Oberon's fairies showed up! They were all little like Mountain Ash, and they flew every which way so we couldn't tell who was who. Coral Bell and Jasmine and Ivy and Forget-Me-Not went to tell Titania, but Algae and I thought you should know, too."

"We saw how you and the princess used to look at each other," said Algae. "It was so romantic! We all thought she was wrong for breaking up with you."

"We didn't exactly break up," said Jak.

"Close enough!" Pansy told him. "So when the other fairies went to see Titania, Algae and I thought we should come see you. We wanted to know if you still feel the same way about the princess, because if you do, we think you should go help her."

Jak climbed out of bed and was shoving things into his backpack when he turned to them long enough to say, "Of course I still feel the same. I'll get her back, don't worry. I'm glad you came to tell me, but I don't understand why you did. Tamisin's mother is queen of the fairies. She has power and abilities beyond anything I can do. Not to mention a lot more resources at her disposal."

"That's just it," said Pansy. "When Titania hears that Mountain Ash took Tamisin, she'll know that Oberon was behind it. Titania will be so angry! She'll send her army to get her daughter back, and there'll be a big fight. People always get hurt when fairies fight. But if someone the fairy king doesn't know were to slip into his forest—"

"And sneak the princess out . . . ," said Algae.

"And take her to Titania . . ."

"So she doesn't send her army into Oberon's forest . . ."

"No one would get hurt."

"Pansy and I have cousins at Oberon's court," said Algae. "We especially don't want *them* to get hurt, which is why we thought that if someone else were to get the princess out before Titania and her army showed up—"

"Everyone would be a lot better off," Pansy finished.

"I see," said Jak. "So you think Mountain Ash took Tamisin to Oberon's forest?" He glanced at the fairies. They were both nodding and looking so earnest that he almost smiled. "And you think I'll be able to sneak in?"

"We used to be one big court before Oberon split off, so everyone knows everyone else, which is why you're so perfect," said Pansy. "Oberon's fairies won't have any reason to suspect a nobody like you. You'll have a better chance of getting in than any of us."

"Gee, thanks," said Jak. Shouldering his backpack, he turned to the fairies. "Anything else I should know?"

Pansy nodded. "The gates are acting weird and no one knows why. There's only one near here that's open right now, and it won't be for long. We'd show you the way, but you'd slow us down. We have to go tell Titania that you're going to help. Maybe then she won't be so quick to send her army."

"You have to hurry and get Tamisin to her mother," Algae added. "Titania has never been known for having a lot of patience."

"Especially when she's mad," said Pansy. "No one gets mad like the fairy queen."

# Chapter 3

Tamisin woke with a start and for a moment thought she was dreaming. It was so dark, she couldn't see anything. Turning her head to the side, she realized there was no pillow beneath her cheek. She was lying on something rigid, definitely not on her soft, comfortable bed. In a rush she remembered what had happened.

Reaching forward, Tamisin felt something grainy and rough almost an arm's length away. It was the same behind her, but when she reached up, there was only empty air. With her hands braced against the surface on either side, she struggled to stand, wobbling as the surface below her feet lurched and bounced. When she fell forward after a particularly bad bounce, she finally gave up, deciding that it might be easier to explore on her hands and knees. Crawling, she worked her way to the point where her path narrowed and she couldn't go any farther. She followed what felt like a wrinkle with her fingers until she jammed her thumb and broke two fingernails.

Tamisin sat back, shaking her hand until the pain of her minor injuries faded. The pain made her angry, and the more she thought about being kidnapped, the angrier she became. When thunder boomed close by and she felt the crackle of electricity in the air, she smiled in satisfaction. Let her kidnapper know that he wasn't going to be able to whisk her away so easily. Whoever had taken her didn't know anything about her. She would call lightning down so that he flew off like a frightened sparrow. In fact, she would do it now, except she didn't know where she was. It felt as if she might be flying. What if her kidnapper was carrying her? If lightning blasted him, they might both die.

The thunder grew fainter as Tamisin sat back and rested her head on her arms. If only she hadn't danced that night! Then Mountain Ash wouldn't have found her and she'd be home in bed while her parents and brothers slept just down the hall. As it was, now they were going to wake up in the morning and find her gone. They would be desperate, not knowing what had happened to her. Considering that the last time she had disappeared, Jak had helped her escape from goblins who wanted to kidnap her, her adoptive family's imaginations were sure to run wild.

Tamisin had no idea how long she sat there, but after what seemed like forever, it felt as if the air pressure was changing. A moment later, she began to slide backward, slowly at first, then faster and faster. Throwing her arms to the side, she tried to stop herself, but it was useless.

Her stomach flip-flopped as she slipped, and what had been the floor suddenly became a wall. There was a loud rasping sound overhead, and the darkness gave way to a pinprick of light that widened enough to reveal a smiling face looking down at her. Tamisin was trying to skitter out of the way when a huge hand blocked the light. Then a finger that looked as big as a tree trunk reached into the bag and poked her. The touch felt as if someone had whacked her with a board. She shot backward and hit the side of the bag.

At first when she began to grow, it was so gradual that she hardly knew what was happening. Then her head poked out of the top of the bag, and she had a moment of panic as the bag grew tight around her. It was getting hard to breathe when she grabbed hold of the sides with both hands and shoved them down until she could squirm out of it like a too-tight dress.

A sea of fairy faces stared down at her. Only one was smiling; the rest were watching her with the same kind of interest that she might have given an unusual insect. It was like a bad dream where everyone knew what was going on except her.

Tamisin was still growing the last few inches when she turned to the smiling face. It belonged to the handsomest man she had ever seen. His black, curly hair brushed the collar of a loose, dark green shirt embroidered with golden leaves. Long, black lashes framed eyes the same green shade as the leaves of an apple tree in the spring.

Tamisin shook her head and looked away. The man's

eyes were hypnotic. When she looked at him again, she focused on his nose. It was a very well-shaped nose, but it didn't make her think of apple trees or spring.

"I thought you might prefer to return to your normal size gradually rather than all at once," said the man in a velvety rich voice. "Some people find a sudden transition too disturbing."

*Even his voice is hypnotic*, Tamisin thought, and found herself leaning toward him to catch his every word.

"I'm Oberon," he said, purring. "I'm your father."

"Oh," she said, too surprised to even try to think of something intelligent to say.

Oberon smiled and Tamisin forced herself to look away. She noticed for the first time that she was in a forest glade alive with movement as tiny fairies came and went. Human-sized fairies dressed in clothes made from flowers and leaves stood facing Oberon. The fairy king was sitting on a seat made of living branches not unlike Titania's throne—Titania, the mother who had given birth to her, then sent her away. The mother whom she didn't really know. Could the fairy queen have lied when she said that Tamisin's father was human? For a moment, joy that her father might really be alive overshadowed her disappointment that her mother might not have told her the truth.

"You must forgive me for taking so long to contact you," Oberon said, "but I've only just learned that I had a daughter. It seems that your mother has been keeping the knowledge to herself. Titania had no right to keep your existence a secret."

Tamisin swallowed hard. This man could make the smallest inflection in his voice sound like a threat, even though she knew he had no reason to threaten her. She glanced at the fairies around him. They were all looking at Oberon as if they, too, had felt his mood change and had frozen, unable to move until they knew what he would say or do next.

When Oberon sat back in his seat and smiled, there was a sound like the rustling of leaves as everyone around him relaxed. "But then my queen likes to keep her secrets. It's one of the many things that I find so charming about her. I want you to live here with me now, something your mother was intent on denying me, I'm sure. It's time you and I got to know each other. You will enjoy living here, as does everyone in my court," he said, and glanced at the fairies closest to him.

They nodded, smiling brightly.

"Wait a minute," said Tamisin. "What makes you think you're my father? Titania told me that my father was a human named Bottom." She would have added that Titania had also told her that Oberon had tricked her into being with Bottom, but she didn't think it was the time to mention it.

The fairies around her gasped. Tamisin doubted that any of them ever questioned Oberon. It made her nervous, too, but she wasn't about to take the word of a stranger over that of the woman she knew was her mother. At least she didn't doubt that relationship. Tamisin looked so much like Titania that anyone could see the fairy queen's claim was true.

Oberon seemed surprised, but instead of being angry, he gave her a half smile and said, "I heard rumors and had my fairies investigate. Your mother told her lies so that I wouldn't send for you. She probably feared that you would turn from her once you knew that I was your father. Come, fairies," he said, gesturing to all the fairies in the glade. "Make my child welcome! See that she has everything she needs. She will live with us now and be a treasured member of our court."

"But I don't want to stay here," Tamisin blurted out. "I have a life back home, and a family, and friends. We had plans—"

"Enough!" Oberon roared, and all the fairies in the glade shrank back. His eyes seemed darker now, more like the green of a fir tree in winter, and his voice was just as cold. "You care more about inconsequential people than you do about the injustice done to me!" the fairy king said in a frightening voice. "How dare you be so ungrateful! I have brought you here to right a wrong that Titania has wrought on us both, and yet you defy me!"

Tamisin didn't like that he was making her feel like a little girl. "I thought you brought me here because you wanted to meet your daughter. If I were meeting my daughter for the first time, I wouldn't start by yelling at her."

Oberon's eyes darkened even more, as did the air in the glade itself. Tamisin wondered if he was about to use some awful magic on her, and even considered apologizing, but suddenly she realized that she didn't care how he felt. She wasn't going to apologize to anyone! He was in the wrong, not her. She was a fairy, too, and could do things she couldn't have even imagined a year ago. If he thought for one minute that he could treat her that way, he had a lot to learn about being a father! Not that she believed he *was* her father. Although no one could deny that she looked like the fairy queen, Tamisin didn't see herself in Oberon at all. And she *had* to be half human. She hadn't even had wings until recently, and hers folded away and were bigger and stronger than those of any full-blooded fairies she'd seen. She couldn't make herself small, either, which seemed to be something that every other fairy could do.

It was so quiet that the entire forest seemed to be holding its breath. The silence continued to grow until suddenly the fairy king chuckled and a breeze wafted through the glade as if even the trees had exhaled. "I like you, child," said Oberon. "You have your mother's fire. I can see why she would want to keep you to herself. So be it. If you truly wish to return to your human home, my fairies will take you back in the morning. In the meantime, they will see that you have the rest and refreshment that you need."

When Oberon looked away and began to talk to the human-sized fairies beside him, Tamisin realized that she was dismissed. She glanced around, wondering where she should go; the sea of faces looking back at her seemed unfriendly, and some even returned her gaze with open dislike.

And then a young man came forward and bowed. Although most fairies appeared ageless, this boy seemed to be about as old as Tamisin. Like everyone there, he had perfect features. Long lashes framed his dark blue eyes, and high cheekbones shaped his narrow face, but he didn't seem as fragile as the rest of the fairies. His body was sturdier, his skin was the same shade of blue as the sky, and his hair was the deep blue of the sea.

"I'd be happy to show you around," he said. "My name is Dasras. We're excited that you're here."

Tamisin thought *he* might be excited, but wondered if that was really true of the others. They seemed more concerned with what Oberon was doing now. The few fairies that glanced at her looked curious but nothing more.

"Can I get you something to eat or drink?" he asked. "We're usually so busy that we don't have formal meals and just eat when we're hungry."

"It has been a while since I ate last," she admitted.

"Then follow me!" he said, and gestured toward a path with a flourish.

She walked with Dasras through the trees to where a spider-silk cloth covered a large, flat rock. Nymphs with long green hair stood on the other side of the rock, pouring a clear pink liquid into cups made from tulip blossoms. As Tamisin and Dasras joined the line of bigger fairies, she accepted a cup from a nymph. "Thank you," Tamisin told her.

Dasras glanced at her in surprise. Tamisin noticed that he didn't say anything when he took the cup from the nymph, nor did any of the other fairies standing in line. Apparently thanking people wasn't normally done at Oberon's court.

A human-looking woman with long, straight brown hair that hung down on either side of her plump-cheeked face was setting a platter of fresh fruit on the rock when she grinned at Tamisin and said, "Be careful. That berry wine will go straight to your head if you're not used to it."

The blue boy frowned at her, saying, "She'll be fine, Irinia."

Ducking her head, the woman turned away. Dasras was helping himself to small brown wafers when Tamisin glanced at Irinia. To her surprise, the woman had an identical face on the back of her head. After scowling at the boy, Irinia glanced at Tamisin and winked even as her other face began to talk to one of the nymphs.

Tamisin looked away when Dasras nudged her and said, "Let's go. I know a spot where we can eat in peace."

*If this is all fairies eat, no wonder they're so slender,* she thought, choosing a ripe plum and a shiny red apple from the platter before following Dasras.

A small flock of goldfinches followed them from tree to tree as they made their way through the forest. Tamisin was listening to their song when she noticed a dull, rhythmic roar that she couldn't quite place. When she and the blue boy entered a clearing at the edge of a rocky outcrop, the sun was low enough in the sky that its light cast long shadows behind them.

"We'll sit up here," Dasras said, and hopped onto the rocks. He was so agile that he reached the top long before Tamisin, who climbed slowly so she wouldn't spill her berry wine. She was working her way from one boulder to another when she realized that the roar was growing louder. Curious, she continued on until she could see over the top of the rocks and stood, stunned, looking out over the vast ocean that lay before her.

Tamisin had never visited an ocean before, and had never smelled the salt air or felt the moist breeze on her face or tasted salt on her lips. She had never seen gulls swooping over the water, skimming the surface as they caught their dinner, or porpoises leaping just beyond the breaking waves.

"Come sit by me," said Dasras, patting the sun-warmed rock beside him.

She climbed across, eager to sit down and drink in the glorious view. The spot Dasras had chosen was at the highest point of an uneven jumble of boulders that fell away to embrace a small cove and the white-sand beach that shaped it. When she looked up, Tamisin could see the sun setting behind the horizon and the endless cycle of waves.

A sense of being at peace came over her, and she realized that for the first time in months, the nagging, almost painful prickling of the thwarted compulsion was gone. She was in the land of the fey; the compulsion was satisfied.

"They say that King Neptune tossed these rocks here to protect his daughters when they came to play on the beach," said Dasras. "I come here often to watch the waves and think. Most fairies don't like the ocean, though. They say the salt water hurts their wings, but I think they just don't like the mermaids."

"Can we go down to the beach?" Tamisin asked, suddenly excited to be there.

Dasras laughed. "I wouldn't advise it. That beach belongs to the mermaids, and the rumors about them are true; they aren't always friendly to strangers."

Tamisin took a sip of her wine and coughed. It was stronger than she'd expected but had a nice fruity taste. "I thought mermaids were usually friendly," she said, and wiped her mouth with the back of her hand.

"None that I've ever met," Dasras said, making a sour face. "So, tell me about yourself. What was your life like before you came here to live?"

"I'm not staying, you know," said Tamisin. "I need to go home. No one knows where I've gone, and they're bound to be worried about me. Jak's the only one who'd be able to find out and—"

"Don't tell me about *them*! I want to know everything there is to know about *you*." He gazed at her so attentively that she couldn't help but feel uncomfortable.

"There isn't much to tell," Tamisin replied. "I learned that Titania was my mother just last year. My friend Jak helped me find her." Juice dribbled down her chin when she took a bite of the plum and the sweet taste exploded on her tongue.

"Jak again!" Dasras said, sounding exasperated. "You

might as well tell me about this Jak. He seems to be important to you."

Tamisin nodded as she swallowed. "He was my best friend, although I guess you could say he was more than that." *Or at least he was until I turned my back on him*, she added silently. When she thought about it like that, she couldn't understand why she'd done it. "I miss him," she said, and sighed.

Dasras gave her a sharp look, then smiled brightly and reached down to pat her hand. "Don't worry. You'll like living here. And I'm sure you'll make plenty of friends."

"I'm not going to live here!" Tamisin cried. "As soon as the sun comes up, I'm going home. Oberon had no right to have Mountain Ash shrink me and stuff me into a bag!"

Dasras's smile faded. "Oberon had him shrink you because it was the safest way to bring you here. And he has every right to see you. He is your father, after all, and Titania should never have lied about you. But then, that's what she does—says one thing when it suits her, then changes her story when the first lie becomes inconvenient."

"What are you talking about?" asked Tamisin.

Dasras shrugged and his expression grew grim. "My mother was one of Titania's handmaidens. She died shortly after giving birth to me, but before she died, she asked Titania to raise me as her own. I was only a year old when Oberon found out about me. He wanted me to live at his court, but Titania refused to give me up. They argued for years over who should keep me, and then one day Titania decided that she wanted to make up with him, even if it

31

meant sacrificing me. They've lived apart for as long as I've known them, but I don't think they ever stopped loving each other."

Tamisin drained the last of the wine from her tulip cup, then said, "And she gave you to him, just like that?"

"She had always told me that I wouldn't be happy living with Oberon, but when it suited her, she changed her story and said that I'd probably enjoy it. She sent me here the very next day, and I've never heard from her since."

"I'm sorry," Tamisin told him. "I have to ask, though. *Are* you happy here?"

Dasras hesitated as if he'd never really thought about it. "Yes, I suppose I am."

"Then maybe something had changed," said Tamisin. "Or you were old enough that she thought you would be all right here. She told me that she sent me away when I was a baby partly because she didn't want to continue fighting with Oberon. I really do believe she sent us away for the sake of the kingdom, not because she didn't want us. I think she probably loved us both in her own way."

Dasras snorted. "Maybe, but she loves the kingdom more."

A bone-jarring shriek split the air as a dark shadow rippled across the water. Tamisin looked up, but all she could see was a shape blocking part of the setting sun.

"We'd better go," said Dasras, getting to his feet. "The griffins are hunting their dinner early tonight. I'll show you to your bed if you'd like. It's going to be dark soon anyway."

"Do griffins hunt fairies?" Tamisin asked, and glanced down at the apple core and plum pit. She didn't remember finishing them off.

Dasras frowned at the remains of the fruit she held in her hand. "You must be hungry after your ordeal. Most fairies don't eat much. And to answer your question, no, they don't usually hunt fairies, but then, fairies don't usually give them the chance."

After Dasras pointed out the place where Tamisin was to sleep, he showed her to a nearby waterfall where she could bathe and then left. When she emerged from the waterfall, a fairy dressed in cobwebs gave her a pale green shift made of woven willow leaves and took away the nightgown Tamisin had been wearing since leaving home.

Tamisin was yawning when she got to her bed and was dismayed to see that it was made of twigs and dangled like a hammock from the branches of an oak tree. She was sure she'd never be able to get any rest, but when she lay down, the moss mattress was so comfortable and the downy cover so soft that she was soon drifting off. A short time later, a light breeze blew in from the ocean, rocking the bed from side to side, lulling her into a deeper sleep.

# Chapter 4

Fairy directions aren't like the kind humans give to each other. Most fairies can't read, so street signs don't mean anything to them.

"Go to the big black path, then go straight until you smell marigolds," Pansy had told Jak. "Turn left at the picture of the black-and-white cow. Go straight until you reach a meadow that a giant could cross in ten strides. Cross the path and go inside the big white cottage. Look for the gargoyle. He'll show you the way to the gate."

With his backpack crammed full of clothes, food, and things he thought might be useful, such as matches and a candle, Jak slipped out the back door. The big black path—fairy-speak for a human road—was only three blocks from his house, so he reached it in a few minutes. Because it was still early, only a few cars passed him, but by the time he reached the downtown area where buildings were closer together, cars were bumper to bumper as people headed to work.

Jak finally smelled the marigolds when he was in front of city hall. He continued down the street until he spotted a fast-food restaurant where a large picture of a cow wearing a sign was displayed on a window. Turning left, he crossed the street and went straight. When he reached a park, he decided that a giant could indeed cross it in ten strides, so he turned again and spotted the big white building that housed the Museum of Fine Art.

A sign in front of the museum said the doors wouldn't open for another hour. Jak sat on the steps and ate a granola bar while he thought about what he would do next. If all went well, the gate would be open and he would soon be in the land of the fey—ideally nowhere near the cat-goblin lands. If the gate had already closed, he'd have to hunt until he found one that was open. There was no telling how long that would take, and the fairies had warned him that he didn't have much time. It would be great if he could take a gate that opened near Oberon, but all the gates around the city opened to places within walking distance of Titania's forest. Gates that led to any other part of the land of the fey would be in another part of the human world, and Jak had no idea where to find them.

When the museum finally opened and a surge of humans headed up the steps, Jak entered the big hall and started searching for a gargoyle. He didn't see any. He did see a fairy couple, although no one else seemed to notice them. A group of people pushed through the revolving doors behind him, jostling Jak as they hurried toward a woman seated at a desk. When he heard them asking the price of admission, he realized that he had to pay to get in. Too bad he hadn't brought any money with him. Where was that gargoyle, anyway?

Jak turned around, ready to ask the fairies where he might find the gargoyle, but the couple had disappeared. Thinking that the creature might be hiding in the museum, he didn't want to ask a human, so he searched the growing crowd, hoping to find another fairy. When his glance fell on a kiosk holding pamphlets, he was surprised to see a gargoyle on the cover. He plucked a pamphlet from the rack, tore off a corner, and held the scrap of paper in his hand while he thought about a ten-dollar bill. Jak was so good at transmogrifying one thing into another that he no longer had to give it much thought. With the money clutched in his hand, he approached the desk and paid the fee, receiving a sticker in return.

"Where would I find this gargoyle?" he asked the woman at the counter, showing her the picture.

"The statue garden," she said, and turned away.

Hurrying to join the line of people waiting to show a guard their stickers, Jak saw a sign only a little farther on. STATUE GARDEN read the sign with a small picture of the gargoyle just above an arrow pointing down another corridor. Jak strode past an elderly couple and turned the corner, almost running into a group of nymphs dressed in leaves and grass. They giggled and looked him up and down. Jak was about to speak to them, but they skipped into the corridor and danced around the elderly couple, who didn't seem to see them.

Jak scowled. Full-blooded fey could make themselves invisible in the human world when there was enough magic around—which there was when a gate was open. He wouldn't have needed to buy a sticker if he could perform that handy little trick, but there were a lot of things that halflings couldn't do.

The statue garden was a large space open to the sky with two ancient oaks dominating the center. Jak was relieved to see that light shimmered between the trees; the gate was open. Directly in front of the trees, the marble figure of a young woman holding an urn stood in a shallow, water-filled pool. Statues of humans in various poses stood around the trees, and a stone gargoyle crouched behind them as if standing guard. Human-sized fairies sat at the feet of the statues or lounged on the edge of the bowl. From the way they kept glancing at the trees, Jak thought they were probably waiting for someone.

A goblin girl with a beak nose was helping an older bird-goblin woman totter toward the exit while three jackal-goblin boys tried to get the girl to talk to them. Jak had known a few jackal goblins at school, all of whom had been nasty friends of his cousin Nihlo. He had avoided them, just as he wanted to avoid these, so he stepped behind a statue and waited for the room to clear.

The light between the trees grew brighter, and a single human-sized fairy appeared. When he stepped into the garden, the group of fairies greeted him, and then gathered up their possessions and started for the door. Jak stepped out of their way, but they still gave him scornful looks and were careful to keep their distance.

"Look, Tansy," said the old bird-goblin woman. "It's a cat goblin. I haven't seen one of those in years. You'd better hurry, young goblin. The light in the gate is getting all waverylike. It's going to close any minute."

"A cat goblin, huh?" said one of the jackal goblins. "And I thought it was just another human. What are you doing here, cat?"

Jak tried to avoid the goblins as he started toward the gate, but they loped across the garden to stand directly in front of him and waited, leering. Out of the corner of his eye, Jak noticed that the bird goblins were using the distraction to shuffle around the corner and out of sight.

"What's the matter? Cat got your tongue?" asked the biggest of the jackal goblins. Like his companions, he had a stocky build and a blunt-nosed face with eyes set too close together. His eyes seemed to merge into one when he shoved his face close to Jak's and snarled. Jak jerked his head back as the goblin's decaying-meat-tainted breath wafted over him. His revulsion must have shown on his face, because the goblin's eyes narrowed as he set his hand on the center of Jak's chest and shoved.

Jak staggered back, then ducked as one of the other jackal goblins took a swing at him. Another step back and he turned and darted behind the statue of a man holding a sword. When the goblins came after him, he wove between the statues at a near run, trying to get closer to the gate. There was a muffled curse, and one of the goblins snapped the head off a spotlight aimed at the fountain, hurling it at Jak. The spotlight missed him, but it hit the statue of a child and bounced off to skitter across the polished floor.

Water began to spout from the marble woman's urn, creating a mist that hid the shimmering light of the gate. A moment later, a human family of four entered the garden. "What is going on in here?" demanded the man. The family looked in horror at the broken piece of metal and glass that lay on the ground at their feet. "Did you just throw that, young man?" the father asked Jak.

"No," he said, then remembered that the humans probably couldn't see the jackal goblins. He glanced behind him and saw the look of glee on the goblins' faces as they realized that the humans *could* see Jak.

"So you're telling me that it got there all by itself?" said the man.

"Avery, let's go," his wife told him as their little girl began to cry.

Jak was trying to come up with something plausible to tell the man when a goblin shoved him from behind. Surprised, Jak went sprawling, but he hopped to his feet in a flash and dodged out of the way as the jackal goblins tried to jump on him.

"What is wrong with you?" the man asked as Jak dodged here and darted there.

Jak was too busy trying to avoid the goblins to worry

about what the man was thinking. He dashed around the fountain and glanced at the trees, but there was so much mist in the air that he couldn't see if there were shimmering lights or not. Suddenly one of the goblins slammed into him and Jak went flying. He hit the statue of the child with a thump, rocking it on its base.

"I'm going to get the guards!" the man declared, and left with his family. They had scarcely left the garden when the goblins descended on Jak again.

"Leave him alone," a deep voice rumbled.

The jackal goblins stopped to look around, then turned back to Jak. "Was that you, cat? You're trying to tell us what to do?"

The grating sound of stone on stone drew their eyes to the gargoyle. It was standing now, and as they watched, it took a step forward even as its stone surface took on the appearance of leathery hide. "I am the guardian of this gate," he said in a voice so low and penetrating that the floor seemed to vibrate. "Leave now, jackal goblins, while you still can."

Jak felt as if his feet had grown roots; he was too terrified to budge. He heard the goblins pelt from the room, but his eyes were fixed on the gargoyle, so he saw when the beast turned its massive, craggy head in his direction.

"Good, they're gone," said the gargoyle in a much less fearsome voice. "I don't like thugs, but there's nothing I can do about them until they break the rules. They never should have gone after you when humans were around. And they broke a light! Do you know how hard I work to make sure nothing draws the humans' attention to this garden?"

"I'm sure you do," said Jak, sounding half strangled. He cleared his throat and added, "I was told you could show me the way to the gate."

"It's right there," growled the gargoyle. "You were just looking at it. See, it's open. You can . . . Aw, heck. The fountain is still on. Just a minute."

The gargoyle's joints creaked as he inched forward. He waved his paw at the fountain and the spray stopped abruptly. Shuffling his feet, the beast returned to his original position and lowered himself into a crouch. "We don't want humans seeing the gate when it's open, so the water goes on when they're in the garden. It makes the shimmery light harder to see."

Jak turned to the trees again; the shimmering lights were back. "Thanks!" he said, and grinned at the gargoyle.

"Hurry," said the gargoyle as his hide turned back to stone. "I hear a large group of humans coming."

Jak's smile broadened as he hefted his backpack higher on his shoulder. He might not know exactly where he was going, but at least now he could get there.

# Chapter 5

The moon was beginning its descent from the night sky when Tamisin dreamed of Jak. He looked much the way he had when she saw him last: his thick black hair tousled and his deep blue eyes darkened with worry as he tried to figure out why she was avoiding him. She felt herself turn away as he swore that he would never stop loving her.

After a time the dream-Jak faded away, and a cloud of fairies dressed in flower colors replaced him. In this part of her dream, Tamisin flew with the fairies, darting over wildflowers and racing across a rainbow. She was enjoying the dream until her bed began to sway and she rose from the depths of sleep. Opening her eyes for an instant, she saw Oberon hovering over her, but it still seemed like part of the dream. Her eyes drifted shut, and she was lingering on the edge of sleep when Oberon dripped flower-scented nectar onto her eyelids, whispering about fatherhood and that she was his daughter who wanted to live at his court and never leave. As she drifted off to sleep again, she felt the nectar and dreamed that someone had kissed her eyelids. The sensation combined with Oberon's words to make her feel warm and loved. Tamisin snuggled deeper under the covers.

Less than a minute later a sturdy figure climbed up the tree trunk and crept along the branch. Tamisin was still dreaming as the blue boy whispered that he was her one true love, and that she was to forget the boy named Jak. When Tamisin rolled over, the boy backed off the branch and down the trunk of the tree, leaving her to a confused dream that made her feel restless and uneasy.

She woke when a tiny bird flitting from branch to branch just above her sang to its neighbors with a warbling trill. Tamisin had a feeling that something had changed, although she didn't know what it might be.

She couldn't wait to spend the day with Oberon and explore his forest. Wiping a strange stickiness from her eyelids, she smiled, delighted that Mountain Ash and Oberon had brought her here. She'd been sure that her biological father was dead, but he wasn't at all, and now she could actually get to know him! Tamisin's heart felt light until it occurred to her that Titania had lied. Who knew what other lies her mother had told her?

This thought made Tamisin angry, souring her good mood. She sat up and looked around. The side of the bed was high enough that she couldn't have rolled out if she'd wanted to, which was good, because when she peered over the edge, she saw that the bed appeared to be about ten feet above the forest floor. It had been dark when she'd finally climbed into it, and she had been so tired that she hadn't even tried to see what was around her.

"Good morning!" called a voice, and Tamisin peered over the edge again. Dasras was there, tossing an apple in the air with one hand. "I brought you some breakfast," he said.

Tamisin's heartbeat quickened and her breath caught in her throat. She ducked out of sight long enough to comb her hair with her fingers and straighten her rumpled shift. "I'll be right down," she called as she opened her wings. Noticing Dasras's admiring gaze as she fluttered to the ground, she blushed, suddenly self-conscious.

"You have beautiful wings," he told her, his gaze as warm as a caress.

"Thank you for saying so," she said, feeling her face flush even redder. Twitching the muscles in her back, she folded her wings and tucked them into the creases between her shoulder blades, aware that Dasras was watching. She'd put them away in front of her parents and . . . someone else she couldn't quite remember, but no one had ever watched her with such intensity before. "And thank you for the apple," she added, taking it from his outstretched hand. Their fingers touched for an instant, and an electric tingle traveled through her arm.

Tamisin glanced up and their eyes met. She swayed toward him, as if drawn by an invisible string, then blinked, shook her head, and stepped back. *What was she doing?* she wondered. She'd just met Dasras the day before!

Dasras smiled and her heart seemed to flutter. "Did you sleep well?" he asked.

Tamisin nodded. "I did, although I had the strangest dreams. I dreamed that . . ." A sudden sharp pain in her foot made her wince and look down. She had shifted her feet when she was talking and stepped on a stone. Although many of the fairies had bare feet, Tamisin didn't think she would be able to walk very far that way.

"Do you know where I can get some shoes?" she asked Dasras, gingerly setting her foot on a patch of bare ground.

"We'll go see the cobbler," said Dasras. "He's only a brownie, but he's very good at his trade."

The look Dasras gave her made Tamisin's cheeks flush again, and she turned away, not sure what to think. He was very attractive and she had the strangest feeling that he was the one for her, but she didn't know why she would feel so strongly so quickly. After all, it hadn't been until she'd gotten to know . . . Tamisin frowned. She was sure that she used to be crazy about someone, but she couldn't remember whom.

"Aren't you going to eat your breakfast?" Dasras asked.

"Of course," she said, and glanced down at the fruit in her hand. Humans had to eat more than just fruit, didn't they? But if both of her parents were fairies, then she was a fairy, too. Tamisin shrugged and took a big bite of the apple. She was just used to eating more; she'd be fine once she'd been there some time.

"Is something wrong?" Dasras asked.

He looked worried about her, which Tamisin thought

was sweet. She gave him her brightest smile and said, "Not at all."

"We should go see the cobbler now. I have a long list of places I want to show you, but you won't get far if you're used to wearing shoes."

Tamisin's eyes lit up. "Is he down by the shore? I'd like to see the ocean again."

"Brownies don't go to the shore," said Dasras with a wave of his hand. "They live on the other side of the briars with the rest of the servants. That's where we're going now. It's just down the hill from the glade where you talked to Oberon yesterday."

"The brownies are servants?" she said, joining him as he began to walk.

"Of course." Dasras gave her a quizzical look. "They aren't fairies, are they?"

"You mean they're servants simply because they aren't fairies?"

"Fairies are the highest class of the fey. Anyone else should be honored to serve them. I know all this is new to you, but everyone . . . Oh, look. There's Buttercup. Let me introduce you."

Buttercup had bouncy blond curls and wore a short dress made of yellow flower petals. Pale green slippers with curved toes covered her tiny feet, and tights the same shade of green covered her legs. She was carrying a woven basket filled with buttercups and seemed to be in a hurry. When Dasras called to her, she turned, her curls bobbing around her shoulders, her blue eyes wide in surprise.

"Dasras! How are you today? And is this the princess? Imagine meeting you here!" Buttercup giggled. "I'm taking these buttercups to Narlayna. I picked them this morning after the dew settled. They're still wet. See!" Plucking a handful of blossoms from the basket, she shook them in Tamisin's face, showering her with droplets. "My gown is about to wilt and Narlayna is making me a new one. Don't you just hate it when your gown wilts? It looks so bad, and everyone thinks you can't take care of your flowers if the petals you're actually wearing dry out."

"Uh, sure," said Tamisin. "That would be awful." It occurred to her that she really didn't know much about being a fairy. She certainly didn't know anything about wilting clothes.

"Oh, dear. Would you look at the time!" Buttercup said, peering through the branches at the sun. "I'm running late. I should have inspected two meadows by now. See you later!" The fairy ran off, leaving a trail of buttercups behind her.

"She seemed . . . nice," said Tamisin.

"I thought you would like her," said Dasras.

They were approaching a stream when a tall, orange-haired fairy wearing an orange gown dotted with black stepped between two thickets. Her expression was sour, and she didn't seem nearly as lighthearted.

"Hello, Lily," Dasras said without much enthusiasm.

"Dasras," she said, acknowledging him with a curt nod. She glanced at Tamisin, and for a fraction of a second Tamisin thought she saw a flash of contempt in the fairy's eyes. "Princess," said Lily before turning back to Dasras. "Are you going to the other side of the briars?"

The blue boy nodded. "We're on our way to see Malcolm about shoes for the princess."

"If you're going there anyway, you can take these to Narlayna," Lily said, holding up a small bouquet of orange tiger lilies. "Tell her to drop whatever she's doing and start this right away. I need a new cap by tonight. I've been away, and my old cap was ruined in a thunderstorm."

"Actually, we—" Dasras began.

"Lily!" called a voice, and a male fairy appeared behind her. "What's taking so long? You know we have to . . . Well, well, what have we here?"

"Dasras seems to be giving the princess a tour," Lily said in a tone that implied she had just tasted something bad. "They're taking my flowers to Narlayna."

"We never said—" Dasras began.

"The princess! We've heard so much about you!" The male fairy snatched the pointed green cap from his head and flourished it even as he bowed. "My friends have neglected to introduce me, so I'll gladly claim the task. I'm Hawthorne," he said, grinning up at Tamisin.

Lily thrust her bouquet at Dasras. "Here! We have to go."

Dasras fumbled and nearly dropped the bouquet. Lily gave him a scornful glance before returning back through the thicket.

Tamisin watched until all she could see of the fairies

was the tip of Hawthorne's cap bobbing above the greenery. "What was that all about?" she asked.

"Shh!" Dasras said softly, holding his finger in front of his lips.

"So," they could hear Lily saying to Hawthorne, "what did you think of her?"

"She's a bit chunky for a fairy, but who am I to say who's a full-blood these days?" said Hawthorne. "There's no denying she's Titania's brat, but as for the rest . . ."

"Oberon will believe what he wants to believe, and there's nothing you or I can say to change that," Lily said, her voice dwindling with distance. "Once he learned that Titania had a daughter, he was convinced that the girl was his child."

Hawthorne's reply was too faint to make out. Tamisin turned to Dasras, who was glaring at the lilies in his hand. "Why do I get the feeling that she doesn't like me?" she asked. "We've never even met before."

Dasras shrugged. "A lot of the fairies in Oberon's court don't think you belong here. Some don't believe that you're really his daughter; others think you might be, but that you've aligned yourself with Titania and have come here to spy for her. Fairies are a very distrustful lot, even of their own kind."

"At least they aren't all as rude as Lily."

"I'd like to say that Lily is the worst of them, but she isn't. At least she's open about the way she feels. Fairies like Hawthorne, on the other hand, will be nice to your face, then stab you in the back if they get a chance. Ah, here we are," Dasras said as he stopped at the edge of a stream. "Let me help you."

Tamisin took his hand and followed him across the water, setting her feet on the large, flat stones that made a path from one side to the other. His hand felt cool and dry, so unlike another hand she remembered holding. That other hand had warmed her own and felt so right that for a time she'd held it as often as she could. And the owner of the hand . . . If only she could remember!

When she looked up, Tamisin saw that they were in a large, well-kept meadow. A tall, thin nymph dressed in fluttering leaves tended to the aspen trees growing alongside the stream. Fairies sat in groups among the wildflowers, talking among themselves until Dasras and Tamisin came close. The fairies grew silent then, and Tamisin could feel their eyes on her as she passed by.

In the center of the meadow, small flower fairies were playing with a dandelion puff, tossing it back and forth between them so deftly that it maintained its fluffy shape no matter how hard they hit it. Dasras and Tamisin skirted the little group, heading for a massive hedge that defined the back of the meadow. As they drew closer, Tamisin saw that it was made completely of briars and was so tall that she couldn't have reached the top even if she'd stood on tiptoe. The wall looked impenetrable from a distance, but Dasras led her directly to a narrow gap in the briars that she didn't see until she was close enough to touch the prickly plants.

"The servants live on the other side of this hedge," Dasras said, stepping into the gap. "Some of them do their work there, and the others have to go back after their work is completed in the fairy side of the forest. There's a curfew at night; they can get in real trouble if they aren't on their side after the curfew."

The hedge was about ten feet thick. Here and there Tamisin could see scraps of fabric and broken twigs where passersby had been unable to avoid the thorns. "Why didn't we fly over this?" she asked, pushing aside a twig.

Dasras glanced back at her. "You could have, but I don't have wings," he said as if it wasn't important. There was an almost imperceptible catch in his voice, however, and suddenly Tamisin understood why he'd looked at her wings the way he had earlier that morning. He hadn't been admiring them as much as wishing he had some of his own.

It hadn't occurred to her that he wasn't a fairy. He was blue, which meant that he wasn't a human, so she'd just assumed that he was a fairy, too. "I didn't mean . . ."

"Narlayna's cave is just through those trees," he said as she stepped out of the briars.

Tamisin stopped to look around, surprised at the differences between this forest and the one on the fairies' side. The other forest had been well groomed, whereas this one had been left in its natural state. Trees grew closer together here, their branches interlaced as they competed for sunlight. Ferns peeped between broken branches that lay uncollected on the ground. Vines grew up the trunks, wrapping themselves around the branches and weighing down the smaller ones. Instead of smelling like masses of flowers, this forest smelled of damp earth and old tree trunks crumbling into decay on the forest floor. It was wild. It was messy. It was exactly the way a forest should be.

"We'll drop Lily's flowers off with Narlayna first," Dasras explained, "then go see Malcolm about your shoes. Don't be afraid when you see Narlayna. She's an ogress, but she won't hurt you."

"I've met ogresses before," said Tamisin. "There are some at Titania's court."

"Hunh" was all Dasras said, but from the look he gave her, Tamisin had the feeling that he didn't want to hear about the fairy queen or her court.

Although the paths weren't lined with smooth pebbles or soft moss as on the other side, enough people had passed through the forest that they had trodden well-defined paths into the forest floor. Tamisin followed Dasras down one such path through a grove of pine trees to a cave set in the side of a hill.

Two large pine trees guarded the path to Narlayna's cave, and they had to go around them to see into the entrance itself. The tall trees cast wide shadows, but just beyond the cool shade the front of the cave was bathed in sunlight, making a cozy spot for the ogress to do her work. They found Narlayna sitting on a stump, her hands flying as she plucked cherry blossoms from a basket to assemble a delicate skirt that looked like flowers floating on a breeze.

Narlayna rubbed her nose with the back of her fingers before raising her head, revealing red eyes and puffy lids. Tamisin thought that she wasn't the least bit frightening. The ogress had brown shoulder-length hair that was blond at the ends, and dark brown eyes that might have looked friendly if she hadn't been so obviously upset. She did have one eyebrow that extended over both eyes, and a few long hairs sprouting from a mole on her cheek, but they weren't anything a good pair of tweezers couldn't fix. If the ogress hadn't been one and a half times the size of a human woman, she might have looked like someone Tamisin could have run across at the mall.

"Lily wants you to make these into a cap for her. She says you're to drop everything and have it ready by tonight," said Dasras, tossing the flowers onto the ogress's lap.

Narlayna's gaze grew hard and cold. "She says that, does she?" she snarled. "Well, you tell her that I'll get to it in my own sweet time! I have two dozen orders before hers, and everyone says theirs is important."

Dasras looked horrified. "I'm not telling her that!"

The ogress sighed. "'Course you aren't. Though it's about time someone did. I'll get to the cap when I can. Just tell her . . . Never mind. No need to tell her anything. She'll get it when she gets it, that's all."

Dasras stomped away, his back rigid with anger, but Tamisin lingered behind. She felt as if she should apologize for Dasras's rude behavior, and for the unthinking demands of the fairy, and for the way they both seemed to treat the ogress. But she didn't know how to begin, so when

Narlayna looked up and snapped, "What do you want?" Tamisin said, "I just wanted to say that you do lovely work," and ran off.

Dasras was waiting for her on the path, looking as if he had something to say, but before Tamisin reached him, a tiny fairy flew down to whisper something in his ear and darted away again.

"I have to go," Dasras told her, his eyes alight with excitement. "Oberon wants me to attend him. He often has me run errands for him or listen when he has a problem to work out. He knows that I can be discreet, unlike most of the fairies here. You'll have to see Malcolm on your own now. Just follow that path and you'll find him."

Tamisin looked where Dasras had pointed and saw the beginning of a faint trail. She had just started toward the path when a flash of red darted past, drawing her gaze after it. It was a cardinal that disappeared into the briars with the barest shiver of leaves. When Tamisin turned around again, she took one step and stopped. The path Dasras had pointed out had ended abruptly.

"He must have meant a different one," she said out loud, and looked about until she spotted another only a few yards on. This path was smoother than the first and easier on her bare feet. It was a meandering route that took her past a gnome carving a chunk of wood who glowered at her when she stopped to see what he was making. A little farther on, a pair of bird-goblin girls were sorting two huge baskets of seeds. They looked up at her approach and turned their backs on her when she smiled at them.

She soon came upon three nymphs standing up to their waists in a small pond scrubbing laundry. "Hello!" called the youngest as Tamisin paused to watch.

"Shh!" said an older nymph. "You're not supposed to talk to them unless they talk to you."

"Why?" asked the young nymph.

"Yes, why?" Tamisin asked.

The two older nymphs looked shocked, but the younger one seemed interested. "Because fairies don't like talking to us if they don't have to," said the nymph whose hair was the darkest green.

"Why is that?" asked Tamisin. The younger nymph turned to her friends as if she, too, were waiting to hear their answer.

"I don't know," said one of the older nymphs.

The other shrugged, saying, "It's always been that way."

"Well, I don't like it," said Tamisin. "You can talk to me whenever you want."

"I'd like that!" said the youngest nymph. Tilting her head to the side, she gave Tamisin an appraising look. "I've never seen you before. Why are you here? No one comes here unless they have a reason."

"I'm on my way to see Malcolm the brownie. I'm going to ask him to make me some shoes."

"Ooh, shoes!" said the youngest nymph. "I wish I could have some shoes."

One of the other nymphs snorted with laughter. "What would you do with shoes? You never get out of the water!"

"You're going in the wrong direction if you want to see Malcolm. The brownies live back that way," said the oldest nymph, pointing at a right angle to Tamisin's path. "Someone should have come with you to take you there. If you keep going on this path, you'll end up in the Land of Forgetfulness and wander there forever."

"Someone was with me, but he was called away. Is there anyone around who can take me to see Malcolm now?" asked Tamisin.

"I can help you," said the youngest nymph. Dipping her hands into the water, she scooped some out and began to shape it into a ball. The water behaved sort of like snow, keeping its shape as the nymph hurled the ball in the direction of Malcolm's home. The ball flew a few yards over the forest floor and stopped almost as if it were waiting.

"Follow the ball. It will take you all the way to Malcolm's house, but you have to hurry," said the nymph. "The water will start leaking soon, and then it will be gone before you know it."

"Thank you!" said Tamisin. "You've been very helpful."

All three nymphs grinned up at her. "You're very welcome," said one.

"Come back and visit us again," said another.

The third just blew her a kiss and waved.

Tamisin was pleased to have a guide, but following the ball wasn't going to be easy. Instead of taking a path, it was going straight through the forest, flying over tree stumps and across a wide gully. Tamisin glanced down at her bare feet, then back at the wild roses growing beside the path. "I am so not doing this," she declared. Shrugging, she released her wings and stretched them behind her.

"Ooh!" she heard the youngest nymph say as Tamisin took to the air.

Following the ball was faster now, and she was glad she was using her wings when she saw the depth of the gully and the jagged rocks at the bottom. She enjoyed darting around trees and over brush that she normally wouldn't have gone near, and in less than a minute the dripping ball had stopped in front of a squat little cottage with a door no higher than her knees.

Tamisin looked around as she landed, but there was no one there to ask if she had indeed reached the right place. When she bent down and rapped on the door with her knuckles, someone inside the house groaned. Loud footsteps tapped across the floor, then wood scraped on wood. Tamisin stepped back when the door swung open, revealing a little man dressed in shades of brown squinting up at her.

"What do you want?" he asked.

"Are you Malcolm the brownie?"

The little man rolled his eyes. "Who else would I be, I'd like to know. Look at me," he said, stepping out of the gloom of his house into the sunlight. Not only were his long-sleeved shirt and trousers brown but so were his fringed boots, his curly hair, his well-trimmed beard, and his deep-set eyes. Tamisin tried not to stare at the hair on the tips of his pointed ears.

"I guess you like the color brown," said Tamisin.

"What? You think I'm called a brownie because I like brown? Does that mean I'd be called a greenie if I were wearing green? No, it does not! I meant look at my size, you big oaf!" he shouted, stamping his foot. "Brownies are little, like me! Oh, I give up. Go away and come back when you've grown a brain."

The little man stomped back to his door and had one foot over the threshold when Tamisin asked, "If you won't make me some shoes, could you at least recommend someone who can?"

The brownie stopped as if he'd been hit with a brick. "Did you say shoes?" he asked without turning around.

"I'm not used to going without them," she said, and held up a bare foot. It was scraped and dirty, and her skin was pale from lack of sun, but at least she'd put on pretty pink nail polish a few days before.

The brownie turned around slowly. His mouth was quivering and he had a glazed look on his face. "Shoes," he breathed and lowered his eyes to her still raised foot. "You want shoes for these?"

Tamisin nodded, then realized he wasn't looking at her face. "That's right. I was told that you could make them for me. That is, if you're Malcolm the brownie."

"Of course I'm Malcolm," the brownie snapped, coming out of his daze. "Have a seat on that stump. I'll be right back."

Tamisin glanced behind her and found a stump beside the path. The top was smooth and the sides had been carved with pictures of shoes. There were pointy-toed shoes and curly-toed shoes, high-heeled shoes and flat-heeled shoes, shoes with ribbons and shoes with buckles, thigh-high boots and light, strappy sandals. Tamisin walked around the stump, examining it from all sides. "Wow!" she said, spotting some delicate slippers with vines for laces that wound up the wearer's legs. "I want those, please!" she said as the little man came out of his house, carrying a basket nearly as big as himself.

"First things first!" he said, setting his basket beside the stump. "Sit down so I can measure your feet." He waited as she took a seat on the stump, tilting his head from side to side as he studied her foot. Then he picked it up and rubbed the dirt off her heel. "Nice foot! Very nice, indeed. I like them big like this, although I've never seen a fairy with such big feet before. And you've obviously used them for walking. Most fairies would rather fly than walk, which is why their shoes last so long."

"Do you make many shoes?" asked Tamisin.

"I used to," the brownie said, sounding wistful. "Before I came here, my shoes were always in demand. I made shoes for every being with feet who wanted to look stylish, but I got so good that Oberon decided I should work only for his court."

"But if they don't have enough work to keep you busy . . ."

Malcolm snorted. "There are two sides to every coin. The fairies want the best shoes for themselves, and they want to keep other beings from having them. You'll never meet a fairy who doesn't think of himself first. They're the most selfish creatures I've ever . . . Uh, sorry! I forgot for a moment that you're a fairy. Your feet . . ."

"Don't worry," Tamisin said. "I'm not offended. And from what I've seen, you're absolutely right."

The brownie gave her an odd look before reaching into his basket. Taking out a knotted string, he held it up to her foot. When the string was too short, he reached into his basket for another that was three times as long. "That's better," he said, pulling the string taut from her toes to her heel. "Are you sure you don't have ogre blood in you?"

"Not as far as I know," Tamisin replied, watching as he wrote something on a leaf he'd taken from the basket.

"Huh," he said, and sat back on his haunches. "I can make you the shoes you picked out, but are you sure you wouldn't rather have a pair like mine?" He held up his own booted foot and waggled it at her, making the fringe flop back and forth.

"No, thanks," Tamisin said, moving her feet out of his reach. "How long do you think it will take you to make them?"

"Not long," he said.

"Tamisin!" a faint voice called.

Although Tamisin couldn't see anyone, she recognized the voice as Dasras's. If she took to the air, she could probably find him easily enough. She glanced at the brownie again, saying, "Do you have all the measurements you need?" When he nodded, she stood and spread her wings behind her. "In that case, I should go. Someone is looking for me. Thank you for the shoes."

Malcolm frowned. "Your name is Tamisin? But isn't that the name of ... Oh, my! You're the one who's supposed to be Oberon's daughter?" He looked at her foot again, and his frown deepened.

"That's right," Tamisin said. "How much will I owe you?"

"Owe me? Why, nothing. The fairies here never pay me for their shoes. It's how I serve the fairy king. Why do you ask?"

"Where I come from, people pay a lot for shoes. Especially ones as nicely made as those," she said, indicating his boots.

"Really?" he asked, his pointed ears pricking up with interest. "And where is that?"

"The human world," she said, and took to the air as his eyes grew big and round.

# Chapter 6

Jak stepped through the gate into the land of the fey and gazed up at the branches swaying high overhead, stealing a moment to enjoy the clean scent of the trees and the open air. He loved the human world, where no one made fun of him for being a halfling, and he could imagine himself spending the rest of his life there, but it was more crowded than the land of the fey and a whole lot dirtier. Not even the parks or undeveloped land in the human world smelled anything like this. With no cars or factories or masses of people gathered together, the land of the fey still smelled the way it always had and, he hoped, the way it always would.

The last time he'd been here he had been with Tamisin, and nothing had gone as planned. She had discovered that her mother was the fairy queen, and he had fallen in love with her, a half-fairy girl. For the first few months after they had returned to the human world, they had been in love and happy. Jak had never fallen out of love, but it seemed that once they argued, Tamisin no longer loved him. She had stopped speaking to him then, and no matter how often he called or tried to talk to her at school, she had refused to listen. Jak had missed her more with each day. Catching glimpses of her in the hallway had made going to school so painful that he had begun to think about returning to the land of the fey to live. Instead, she had gone there without him. Jak was worried not only for her safety but because he had no idea how she would react when she saw him.

He was headed downhill when he came across a trickling stream with water so clear that he could see silver-scaled fish darting among the rocks. Thirsty, he bent down and cupped his hands, scooping up water to drink. He was still bent over when he noticed that a reflection had appeared in the water beside his. Sunlight was glinting off the water just enough to make it hard to see, but then he realized what it was and his head snapped around. A leering wolf goblin stood behind him, only a few feet away. His hair was silver, but his face looked only a few years older than Jak's.

"Look at what I found, boys!" the wolf goblin said over his shoulder. "A cat goblin! I haven't chased a cat goblin in ages."

Another young wolf goblin appeared from behind a massive trunk on the opposite side of the stream. His eyes seemed to glow golden even in the shadows of the trees. "None of us have. Not since before Wulfrin made a pact with the leader of the cat-goblin clan."

"But that pact was dissolved when your leader made a treaty with Titania," the silver-haired goblin told Jak. "And that means that you're fair game again."

Jak rose to his feet as a third wolf goblin padded up to him. The goblin's nose twitched as he sniffed Jak, then raised his head to sniff the air. "He's alone."

The silver-haired goblin, who seemed to be the leader of the pack, reached out and prodded Jak with a claw-tipped finger. "Run, cat boy! Maybe you'll even get away!"

"For a little while!" called the golden-eyed goblin as he took a step closer.

Even as Jak took off running, the pack leader shouted, "Give him a minute. It's more fun if they have a head start!"

Jak ran. Wolf goblins weren't known for treating their victims kindly, and the younger ones were rumored to be the worst. Jak was faster than most humans, and had learned long ago when to stand and fight and when to run. He might even have a chance at outrunning the wolf goblins if there weren't so many of them. He'd seen only three, but he caught glimpses of others running through the trees on either side of him. Each time he tried to change direction, another one would jump out, forcing him back the way they obviously wanted him to go. When that happened, Jak tried to run faster, hoping to get ahead and pass them, but he never seemed to run fast enough. He thought about climbing a tree, but then he'd be trapped, and he didn't have time to waste. He had to move quickly if he wanted to reach Tamisin before Titania started a war. Getting her daughter back might be the only thing that would keep the fairy queen from attacking.

A change in the air alerted Jak that the edge of the forest was near. He could feel a breeze now, carrying the scent of sun-warmed grass and wildflowers. The air was warmer, too, and the trees weren't quite as old or as tall. And then he found himself out in the open with the trees behind him and a sea of grass beginning only yards away.

The wolf goblins rushed to cut him off, but Jak plunged into the Sograssy Sea before they could close their circle. The goblins whined, milling around in confusion, surprised that he would dare to enter the tall grass. Jak had reached grass almost as high as his head when the leader of the wolf goblins gave a short bark and the pack dashed into the sea after him.

When Jak glanced back and saw that the goblins were still chasing him, his heart skipped a beat. Because of the lamias who lived in the Sograssy Sea, few other creatures dared to enter it, but Tamisin and Jak had befriended one of the lamias and no longer feared the seemingly endless sea of grass. Most goblins would give up rather than chase anything past the shore, but these goblins continued to thrash through the grass behind him.

Jak was tired of running, but the wolf goblins kept after him. Although his long, loping stride normally could carry him far, he couldn't go on indefinitely. Soon he would need to stop, and to do that he was going to need help. "Lamia Lou!" he shouted as he forced his way through a thicker stand of grass. "Lamia Lou!" he shouted again as the sounds of the wolf goblins grew louder behind him.

Jak wondered where his friends were. The grass in front of him began to wave wildly, but instead of the face he hoped to see, a wolf goblin popped into sight. Jak staggered to a halt as another goblin appeared a few yards to his left.

*I need to make noise*, he thought as the wolf goblins formed a circle around him. He needed to be loud and he needed to sound bad, so Jak decided to sing. Most cat goblins have terrible singing voices, and Jak was no exception. The first song that popped into his head was a cat-goblin lullaby, the only song he remembered his mother singing to him when he was a kit. It was meant to be sung softly, but Jak opened his mouth wide and screamed it as loudly as he could.

*Sleep tight, little one*
*Curled up toes to nose*
*Slow-winged birds and plumpish mice*
*Fill your tummy—oh so nice.*
*Pleasant dreams will soothe your sleep*
*I'll be here so you can keep*
*Sleeping tight, little one.*

The wolf goblins howled with laughter. "Are you trying to put us to sleep, cat boy?" shouted the leader.

The grass behind him began to rustle. Expecting a wolf goblin to tackle him at any moment, he was halfway through the song again when something large and leathery swiped at his legs and knocked his feet out from under him. He could hear the frightened yipping of the wolf goblins and the thud of their bodies hitting the ground even as he lay on his back, staring up at what he could see of the sky. The next thing he knew, a beautiful female face was glaring down at him. Her hair was russet brown, her eyes were emerald green, and her nose and mouth were perfectly formed. Sparkling jewels dangled from the gold chains that encircled her slender neck, and she smelled like musk and sandalwood. Silky fabric covered her from collarbone to waist. The only things that Jak didn't like were the two fangs revealed when she curled her pink upper lip. She was a lamia; though she looked like a lovely young human woman from the waist up, she had the body of a snake from the waist down.

Jak gulped as yellow drops of venom formed on the tip of each fang. The lamia was already leaning toward him when he cried, "Wait! I'm a friend of Lamia Lou's! Don't you remember me? She introduced us when you helped Princess Tamisin!"

The lamia tilted her head and examined him. Suddenly recognition lit her eyes. Making a sucking sound, she drew the venom back into her fangs before covering them with her lip. "I remember you! Hey, Lamia Lee," she called, "thith one'th a friend of Lamia Lou'th! Come over and thay hi!"

"I'll be right there!" another lamia called. Jak could hear her say something to the wolf goblins, then the sound of thrashing as they tore through the grass, heading out of the Sograssy Sea.

It was obvious that the two lamias were sisters; the second was as beautiful as the first and wore just as many gold necklaces. "I'm Lamia Thlamia," lisped the one who had knocked Jak to the ground.

"And I'm Lamia Lee," said the other one, holding on to Jak's hand until he was on his feet. "You were with the printheth, weren't you?"

"That's right," said Jak.

"What are you doing here?" asked Lamia Shlamia.

"I was looking for Princess Tamisin when those wolf goblins found me," he said, nodding toward the fleeing goblins. "Thanks for coming by just now. I'm sorry I made so much noise, but it was the only thing I could think of that would get your attention. Is Lamia Lou around? I really need to talk to her."

It had occurred to Jak that he might be able to get to Tamisin more quickly if he had help. Should any more goblins show up, they wouldn't think of bothering someone with a lamia at his side.

"I think Lamia Lou ith thtill at home," said Lamia Shlamia.

"We can take you there," Lamia Lee added. "Lamiath don't have many friendth, and the oneth we do have are thpecial. Too bad you didn't tell me about thothe goblin boyth before I let them go. I thought they were friendth of yourth."

Jak shook his head. "I'd never met them before."

"You thould have theen how thcared they looked!" chortled Lamia Lee. "They actually thought I wath going to bite them!"

"Imagine that!" Jak said, glancing sideways at Lamia Shlamia, who blushed and ducked her head.

The lamias' home was in the center of the Sograssy Sea, hidden beneath the grass. Jak didn't see the opening at first; there wasn't even a hill, let alone a door. The ground was as flat and level as the rest of the sea, with nothing unusual to distinguish it from the waving grass around it, and he wondered how they could tell that they were home. When he asked them, they both shrugged.

"It smells like home," said Lamia Lee.

"Really?" said Jak. Although he'd always thought he had a fairly decent sense of smell, this part of the sea smelled like any other to him. Then again, he wasn't wriggling on his belly, nose-deep in the grass.

"We go in over here," Lamia Shlamia said, bending down to dig her fingers into the dirt. When she stood, she was holding the lip of a trapdoor and Jak could see a faint light illuminating the underside of the wood. "After you," she said.

"Actually, I think I'll let you go first," said Jak. He wasn't sure what to expect and thought it might be better if he could watch how the lamias went in.

Lamia Lee went first, ducking her head and slithering in on her belly. When her sister followed her the same way, Jak realized that he hadn't learned a thing by watching them. Still not sure what to expect, he knelt beside the opening and peered in. He could see the ground below, but the light was so dim that he couldn't tell how far away it was or what might lie beyond it.

"Come on!" said Lamia Shlamia, reaching through the opening and grabbing the collar of his shirt. With one powerful jerk, she yanked him off his knees and into the hole. He was kicking out, trying to find something he could stand on, when the lamia set him gently on the ground.

Jak stumbled and nearly fell. He was in a wide tunnel that would have been big enough to drive a car through in the human world. It had rounded sides that reflected light at odd angles. When he put his hand up to steady himself, he felt something rough and realized that the walls were encrusted with old scales, rubbed off passing lamias. The only source of light seemed to come from crystal jars filled with a glowing, swirling gas. When he started to walk, Jak discovered that the floor was also rounded and made smooth by the passage of heavy snake bodies over hundreds of years.

Although he would have liked to have taken his time to look around, the lamias were already slithering down the tunnel. Jak followed them for nearly ten minutes before he saw another, even brighter light up ahead, and heard some familiar voices.

"You brought *whom* with you?" Lamia Lou asked.

The clop of hooves was loud on the stone floor, and Jak was delighted to see Herbert waiting at the end of the tunnel. The white unicorn twitched his ears and made a funny puttering sound. "What are you doing here?" Herbert asked. "I thought you went to the human world with Tamisin."

"I did," Jak said. He waited as Lamia Lou spoke to her sisters. When they were finished, the two lamias who had brought him turned and waved, then left by another tunnel. A fourth lamia remained behind, cradling two blanket-wrapped bundles in her arms.

"Is Tamisin here, too?" Herbert asked, peering up the tunnel.

"No," Jak told him. "Although she is in the land of the fey. One of Oberon's fairies kidnapped her. I'm on my way to Oberon's forest to get her back."

"Why were wolf goblinth chathing you?" Lamia Lou said to Jak as she slithered up to drape an arm across Herbert. The unicorn leaned against her, wuffling softly. "What'th going on, Jak?"

Jak shrugged. "Apparently the wolf goblins no longer feel they have to honor the pact they had with the cat-goblin clan."

"I'm not thurprithed," said Lamia Lou. "Thingth are getting a little crazy around here. I've heard that the wolf goblinth and at leatht two other clanth are up to their old trickth again, terrorizing villageth and waylaying travel-erth. Before you go anywhere, we thould find out whatth going on. Why don't you thtay with Lamia Lynn while Herbert and I do a little invethtigating? We know thome-one who keepth track of all that kind of thtuff."

"I have to get going," Jak said. "Tamisin needs me and I—"

Lamia Lou patted his back, saying, "Don't worry, we won't be gone long."

"I don't think I—" Jak began, but the unicorn and the lamia were already heading for another tunnel.

"Would you like thomething to drink?" Lamia Lynn asked as she laid one of her bundles in a long woven basket. "I have thome delithiouth fruit juithe that I thqueezed mythelf."

"That would be nice," said Jak.

"Here, you can hold Lamia Norelle while I get your drink. I'll be right back."

"What? I don't know how to . . . Oh!" Jak exclaimed as she handed him the other bundle she was carrying, positioning it in his arms. He looked at the tiny head cradled against his chest and suddenly didn't know what to say. A little human face gazed up at him with vivid blue eyes, her face framed in soft brown curls.

Lamia Lynn chuckled as she left the room, Jak watching her with both surprise and dismay. When he glanced back down, the baby's eyes were fixed on his face. Suddenly her tiny mouth puckered and her bright eyes clouded over as if she was about to cry. When the first sob shook her little body, Jak jiggled her and began to walk, saying, "Now, now, your mother will be right back."

The baby grew silent for a moment, but only because she was drawing a deeper breath. And then the wailing began and Jak really didn't know what to do. He walked the length of the room, jiggling her gently. When the wailing got louder, he walked faster and began crooning nonsense words, hoping to distract her.

"Burp her," said the baby's mother as she set a glass of something pale green on the closest table.

"I don't know how," Jak said, and handed the baby over. He watched as the lamia turned the baby to her shoulder and began to pat her back with forceful little thumps. The baby wiggled and the blanket that had been wrapped around her came loose, falling to the floor and freeing a long snake tail that had been wrapped up inside. Soon a loud burp emerged from the little girl, and both mother and child looked satisfied.

Lamia Lynn glanced down at her shoulder and laughed. "You mutht feel better now! You thpit up all over uth both. Come along, my darling. We need to get cleaned up. I'll be right back," she said, turning to Jak. "Pleathe, make yourthelf comfortable."

Left by himself, Jak's gaze wandered around the cavernous room that somehow had a cozy feel to it. The crystal jars dotted the walls in a flowing, swirling pattern, both lighting the room and decorating it. Long, low cushions covered with brightly colored fabric made of woven grass lined the floor by the walls, perfect for reclining lamias. Tables of various heights were set around the room, some holding quill pens and parchment, others supporting stacks of books, some of which looked familiar. He wondered if the lamias ever went through the gates to the human world.

Jak yawned, worn out from a very long day. He took a seat by a table covered with books and picked up one at random. While thumbing through the book, his eyes closed and his head lolled back. Only a few minutes after sitting down, Jak was snoring.

It seemed only moments later that Jak woke to a raccoon goblin shaking him so hard that his head thumped against the wall behind him and the book he'd been holding slipped to the floor. Annoyed, he sat up and pushed away his old school friend's fur-covered hand.

"We found him!" Herbert announced. "He knew all about it."

Tobi hopped up onto the seat beside Jak. "I'm surprised to see you here, Jak! I've heard that the gates are acting all squirrelly—opening for a little while, then closing so fast hardly anyone knew they were open at all. Seems just about nobody's coming through lately. But that's enough about you. I've been busy since you left, Jak. I'm in the information business now. After Titania made me spy on you, she decided that I was pretty useful and had me keep an eye on some other people, too. I got real good at it, so now I have a network set up all over the place. I have eyes and ears everywhere."

"He means he has lots of relatives scattered around," said Herbert. "They can't stand living close to each other, so they live all over the place."

"Huh," grunted Tobi. "Anyway, I've been cultivating my connections lately."

"He visited his grandmother and saw his cousins and made up with his brother Yardley, whom he had a big fight with a few years ago," Herbert explained. "He told us about it on our way here."

"My relatives aren't my only informants! I have others . . . ," Tobi said, glancing around the cave as if he expected to see one.

"So what have you heard about Tamisin?" Jak asked.

"I was just getting to that," said Tobi. "She's here, all right, although she's not *here*, if you know what I mean. Mountain Ash took Tamisin to Oberon's court. Rumor has it that the fairy king thinks she's his daughter. Titania thinks Oberon did it just to get at her, so she's madder than I've ever seen her. Last I heard she was preparing her troops to head to the shore of the Southern Sea where the fairy king's court has been living."

"I need to get to Tamisin as soon as I can," said Jak.

"I'll go with you, ole buddy," Tobi announced. "Two heads are better than one. Unless you're a troll, and then they're half as good as one."

"We can take you part of the way," offered Lamia Lou. "Can't we, Thweetie?"

"Of course we can, Sugar Lips," said Herbert.

"How far is it from here?" asked Jak.

"Jutht a minute," Lamia Lou said. "I can thow you." She left the room and was soon back holding a piece of yellowed parchment. "Here we go. Thith map uthed to belong to my grandmother, but thingth can't have changed much. Thith ith where we are," she said, pointing to the large green spot on the map labeled Sograssy Sea. "And thith ith where Oberon'th court ith." Her finger traced the uneven outline of a section marked "Oberon's Forest" just above the wavery lines of the ocean.

"What's that?" Jak asked, pointing to a line that ran from one side of the map to the other.

"That'th the Great Ditch. Herbert and I can take you that far, but after that you'll be on your own."

Herbert nodded. "The ditch has really steep sides, and I can't climb. The Roaring River is at the bottom of the ditch, and Lamia Lou can't swim."

"I can climb and swim!" Tobi declared. "Don't worry, Jak. I'll stick with you. I always do!"

Jak glanced down at his little friend and sighed. He remembered all the times he'd counted on Tobi and the little goblin had run off. He wasn't so sure how much help Tobi would be.

"Onthe we leave the Thograthy Thea, we have to make a choith," said Lamia Lou, tapping the map with her finger. "Dragon Territory is full of dragonth, tho no one goeth that way. Rockth are alwayth crathing down from the Trembling Peakth, tho that way ith too dangerouth, too. I thuggetht we go through the Griffin Hunting Groundth. Griffinth are afraid of lamiath; we thould be thafe there."

"What about after we cross the ditch?" asked Jak. "You won't be with me then."

"You'll have to choothe between Troll Woodth, Thphinx Alley, or the Land of Forgetfulneth."

"Troll Woods are full of trolls so stupid that they're really dangerous," said Tobi. "And no one knows what a sphinx will do. It's impossible to tell what they're thinking. I vote we go through the Land of Forgetfulness. I've heard that you'll forget where you're going unless you write it down, but if you do, it's the safest route to take. Here, take a pencil and a piece of parchment." The little goblin scurried across the room and took what he needed from a table.

"Then that's how we'll go. Thanks for all your help," Jak said, turning from Lamia Lou to Herbert.

"Any time, ole buddy," said Tobi. "Any time at all."

# Chapter 7

Dasras was off on another mission for Oberon when Malcolm brought Tamisin her new shoes. Tamisin was surprised that he had finished them so quickly. She picked them up to examine them, half expecting hurried and shoddy work. But although they looked as delicate as newly opened rosebuds, Tamisin was delighted to see that they were sturdy and well made.

"So are you just going to stare at them like some gap-jawed fish or are you going to try them on and see how they fit?" asked the brownie.

"Do you talk to all fairies that way, or just me?" Tamisin asked as she sat down and pulled on one of the slippers.

Malcolm grunted. "I don't generally talk to fairies."

Tamisin glanced at him, expecting to see a smirk on his face, but he looked as if he was serious. "Why not?"

"Because I can't stand 'em. Most fairies are either conceited idiots or just plain idiots. But if you ever tell anyone that I said that, I'll deny it with my last dying breath."

"And I'm not an idiot?" Tamisin asked as she wrapped the vinelike laces around her leg.

"Not as bad as most," he replied. "You're different."

"I know. It's my big feet, isn't it?"

The brownie snorted. Tamisin had a feeling it was the closest he ever came to laughing. "It's not the size of your feet I'm talking about. It's the size of your heart. I think you have one, and I can't say that about most fairies. There's something else about you, though. I'm trying to figure out what it is."

A shadow fell over Tamisin and she glanced up. It was Irinia, and she looked as surprised to see Malcolm as Tamisin had been. "What are you doing here?" the woman asked the brownie.

Tamisin held up the shoe she had yet to put on. "He brought my new shoes. Aren't they beautiful?"

"They're lovely, Your Highness," said Irinia, looking even more surprised.

Grumbling to himself, Malcolm stomped off, leaving Tamisin and one of Irinia's faces staring after him. "What an odd little man," said Tamisin. "He says the strangest things."

"Malcolm talked to you and he wasn't insulting?" Irinia asked.

Tamisin nodded.

"This is a first. I've never known him to leave the other side of the briar hedge, let alone hold a conversation with someone. He must really like you."

"Please sit down," said Tamisin, patting the ground

beside her. "I'd enjoy your company. And you don't need to call me Your Highness."

Irinia took a seat on the grass beside Tamisin, sighing as she sat down. "It feels good to get off my feet. I was due a break, so I thought I'd come see you and ask if you have everything you need. I know fairies aren't very good about that kind of thing; they rarely think of anyone but themselves. Do you need anything?"

"I'm fine, thank you," Tamisin told her. "Dasras has been taking care of me."

"What do you think of our blue boy?"

"He's very nice," Tamisin replied, not sure how much she should say. She'd had conflicting feelings about Dasras all day, although she wasn't sure why. Then Tamisin thought of a question she'd been dying to ask someone. "I thought Dasras was a fairy, but he said he isn't. What is he then? I mean, he's blue, so he can't be a regular human."

"I've heard that he's the son of a demigod. Oberon adopted Dasras when the boy was little."

"So I heard. If he's the son of a demigod, does Dasras have any special abilities?"

"None that I know of. He thinks he has a way with girls, but he really doesn't. Listen, before I go back to work, there's something I wanted to tell you. Doing the kind of work I do, I hear a lot. Fairies tend to take the nymphs and me for granted and sometimes forget we're there. Anyway, be careful. Most fairies can't be trusted at the best of times, and you've had enemies since the moment word got out that you existed. The fairies at Oberon's court are very competitive. Because you're his daughter, he's bound to give you the attention they've been fighting over for years, and you won't have to do anything to get it but be yourself."

"Why are you telling me this? You really don't know me."

Irinia shrugged. "You remind me of my nieces. My twin sister married a human. They live in a place called New Jersey. I've been to visit them a few times, and I'm crazy about the kids."

"You mean your sister is able to pass as a regular human?"

Irinia snorted. "Are you kidding me? It's so easy! Look . . ." Turning around so her back was toward Tamisin, the woman squeezed her eyes shut, ran her fingers through her hair, and pulled it over the face on the back of her head. "A lot of my people go to the human world. We're big fans of ice cream and television, and most of my family loves the Yankees. You know how people say someone has eyes in the back of their head? You'd be surprised how often it's true! Anyway, I've got to go, but remember what I told you. Be careful!"

Irinia stood and was about to leave when Tamisin spoke up. "There is one thing: I was wondering when I'd be able to see my father again. Dasras said Oberon would send for me when he wants to see me. Should I wait for a messenger, or should I just go see him on my own?"

"If I were you, and it was my father," said Irinia, "I'd go see him regardless of what anyone told me. But fairies are different, so . . ."

"Thanks," Tamisin said, getting to her feet. "I think I'll do just that. Do you know where I would find him at this time of day?"

"Probably in the glade where you first saw him. He'd be listening to petitioners right about now."

Tamisin enjoyed her walk through the woods, even if she was by herself. She hadn't wanted to come to the fairies' world, but now that she was back, she was excited to see what each new day brought. Oberon was her father, which meant that she was a full-blooded fairy, and it was here, in the land of the fey, that she should feel most at home. Smiling, she hugged herself from sheer happiness, delighted that she finally knew where she belonged.

She was in such a good mood that she started to skip, but hadn't gone far when she spied a cluster of daisies growing by the side of the path. Tamisin bent down to touch a velvety petal and was startled when a fairy dressed in the same yellow as the daisy darted out of the flowers like an angry bee.

"Just what do you think you're doing?" the fairy demanded, her pink cheeks turning red with anger. "You were going to pick one of my flowers, weren't you? I bet you're one of those people who picks every flower she likes. The nerve!"

"I wasn't going to—"

"And picking it while I was inside, dusting it with pollen!"

"I didn't know you were there," Tamisin replied. "And I wasn't going to pick it."

"Yeah, like I believe that!"

Tamisin sighed and started on her way again, no longer quite so excited. "At least at home no one jumps out of flowers at you," she murmured to herself, and wondered how long she would think of the human world as home.

A lilting melody drifted through the trees. Curious, Tamisin followed the song to the glade where a satyr was playing pan pipes while a pair of nymphs clacking finger cymbals skipped around the fairies waiting their turn to speak to the fairy king. A small group of fairies was standing in front of the fairy king, listening to him with rapt attention. They all looked serious, as if they were discussing something very important. Oberon's expression made him seem formidable.

Tamisin wasn't sure what to do. Should she join the waiting fairies or approach Oberon directly? After all, he was her father and had brought her here so they could get to know each other, but if he was busy, maybe this wasn't such a good time. She finally decided to stay where she was until most of the fairies had gone and he might actually have time to spend with her. While she was waiting, she could look for similarities between the two of them.

She noticed right away that Oberon gestured when he spoke. She did that, too. So did a lot of people, but not as much as Oberon and not with so much emphasis. He also angled his head toward the person who was talking, something she didn't do, nor did she lift one side of her mouth more than the other when she smiled. Oberon's movements were distinctive and solely his. Tamisin didn't recognize any of herself in what he did.

She had been there only a few minutes when Oberon's eyes drifted in her direction. With a gesture and a softly spoken word to the fairies, he ended their conversation and dismissed them. Leaning forward on his throne, Oberon beckoned to Tamisin. "What brings you here, dear child?" he asked once she had joined him. "Was there a boon that you wanted me to grant you? A gift, perhaps?"

Tamisin shook her head. "I don't want anything from you. I just want to get to know you."

"Really? How interesting," said the fairy king. "You were watching me quite intently. Were you looking for something in particular?"

"I was looking for ways that I might be like you, but I haven't seen any yet. Do you suppose we might like the same kinds of things? I like dancing and gardening and visiting museums. My favorite food is caramel popcorn, and I like any music with a beat I can dance to. What about you? What do you like?"

Oberon quirked an eyebrow in surprise. "You want to know what I like. No one has ever asked me that before, at least not the way you mean it. Well, I like pan pipe music and the sound of fairies laughing. I like the color green, but then so do most fairies. I like the tangy taste of frillet berries touched with dew and the way the forest smells after a gentle rain. And I like that you asked me this question," he said, giving her the warmest smile she'd seen him give anyone.

A fairy in the crowd coughed, and Oberon looked up, his smile fading. He sighed and turned back to Tamisin. "I would like to continue our talk, but I seem to have more petitioners than usual. Why don't you stay while I complete my business for the day? You may watch me as long as you wish. Perhaps you'll learn something more about me."

Tamisin stepped to the side, passing the fairies waiting to speak to Oberon. They glared at her as if she had jumped the line at an amusement park. "There aren't too many here," she muttered, thinking it wouldn't take too long, but she'd been standing there only a few minutes when another group of fairies entered the glade.

"You don't need to stay if you don't want to," said a voice. It was Dasras; she was relieved to see a friendly face. "Oberon has probably already forgotten that you're here. Come walk with me and I'll show you around some more."

Tamisin was reluctant to go, but because it looked as if Oberon would be busy for quite some time, she decided that she might as well leave. She walked to the path with Dasras, thinking about all the things she would like to do with her father and wondering if he would ever have the time to do them. When her adoptive father had brought work home from the office, he had always set it aside when

Tamisin or her brothers wanted to talk or play catch or go for a walk. Of course, *he* hadn't been a fairy with all the responsibilities of a king.

Dasras paused to pick a daisy growing beside the path. "A blossom for your thoughts," he said, handing Tamisin the flower.

"I was thinking about my father. Do you suppose he'll ever have time to do things with me? I mean, I thought he wanted to get to know me, but he's so busy and . . ."

Dasras no longer looked interested so much as annoyed. "He is the king," he said, sounding impatient.

"Yes, I know, but he brought me here, and I thought he'd try to spend some time with me. I don't know, the whole thing has me so confused. I was sure he wasn't my father, but now I'm sure he is, yet I don't look like him at all, and when I try to talk to him . . . Am I boring you?" she asked. While she'd been talking, Dasras's eyes had glazed over, and she knew he had stopped listening to her. She'd never had anyone ignore her quite so blatantly before. It irritated her at first, then started to make her angry.

Dasras glanced at her and finally noticed her expression. "What's wrong?" he asked.

"You weren't listening to me, were you?"

"Sure I was," he told her. "Your father . . . Confused . . . I heard you. I have something that will take your mind off all that. Come here." Turning to face her, Dasras pulled her into his arms and pressed his lips against hers.

Something in Tamisin told her that this was good, that

this was the way it should be because he was her true love, but the rest of her was angry. If he loved her, he wouldn't want to cut her off like this; he'd actually care about what was bothering her.

"Don't," she said, putting her hands on his chest and pushing him away.

"But why?" he asked as he tried to pull her close again. "I know you love me. You want this kiss as much as I do."

Hearing this, Tamisin wondered why she had ever thought she might love him, and the little voice that said she did grew fainter. "How could I love you? I barely even know you! What have I ever said that would make you think I love you?"

Dasras let go of her arms and stepped back. "But you have to love me! It always works for . . . Never mind. I guess I was wrong."

"You bet you were wrong," Tamisin said, rubbing her arms where he'd dug his fingers into her flesh. "Why did you say that I *have* to love you? I don't *have* to do anything! And what did you mean, it always works? What are you talking about, your smooth approach? If that's the way fairies do things around here, I don't like it!"

"I'm sorry," Dasras said, looking embarrassed. "I guess it was a misunderstanding."

"I'd say!" said Tamisin. "I think I'll skip that tour now."

"I said I was sorry! Listen, there's a dance tonight. Actually there's a dance almost every night. I was going to ask if you wanted to go with me this evening."

Although Tamisin usually welcomed any reason to dance, she wasn't in the mood for it tonight. All she wanted to do was be alone to think. Besides, what if she danced and her mother's fairies were drawn to her? She had no desire to see her mother just then, not after learning that Titania had lied to her about her father. But she didn't feel she could share that with Dasras. He was acting strangely, and she had no desire to explain herself to him.

"Not tonight," replied Tamisin. "I'm awfully tired."

"Tomorrow night, perhaps?" he said, looking hopeful.

"Maybe," she told him. But she didn't think she would.

# Chapter 8

Morning mist still lingered in the dips and hollows when Jak and his friends started out. Tobi sneezed as he scampered ahead while the others followed more slowly. When he came back, the fur on his head and arms was damp.

The sun was just beginning to burn away the mist when Jak adjusted his backpack. "I've been thinking," he said to Tobi. "Oberon taking Tamisin like this is the worst possible thing that could happen right now. The goblins are restless and Titania needs Oberon's support more than ever, but kidnapping Tamisin was bound to drive a wedge between them. It wasn't like it was a friendly invitation."

"That's true," piped up Tobi. "Rumors say that Titania's furious, which is why I'm not going anywhere near her."

"The fairy queen will never thtop until the hath Tamithin," Lamia Lou said. "I can't blame her, though. I would do the thame thing if it were my daughter."

Herbert snorted. "Even after she gets Tamisin, she won't ever forgive Oberon. This is so much worse than that time they fought over that blue boy."

"Everyone who doesn't like fairy rule would be happy," said Tobi. "There'd be chaos again, just like there was before Titania and Oberon took control."

"There won't be any fighting if I can get Tamisin back to her mother fast enough," said Jak. "I just have to get there before Titania's army starts the first battle."

They were well into the hills of the Griffin Hunting Grounds when Tobi began to whine. "Can I ride on your back?" he asked Herbert. "I'm tired and my feet hurt."

"No!" said the unicorn. "What do you think I am, a horse?"

Tobi ran around Herbert to walk beside Lamia Lou. "Then how about you?" he said. "I know you give people rides."

"Only thertain people," she replied. "And you're not one of them."

Tobi pouted, but a moment later he was skipping along next to Jak, looking up at him with big pleading eyes. "Jak, could you—"

"No," said Jak. "I'm not carrying you."

"But I had to walk all the way to the Sograssy Sea just to talk to you, and now you're making me walk all the way to—"

"No one is making you go," Jak told him. "You could always turn around and go home."

"Huh," Tobi grunted.

It wasn't long before the little goblin disappeared over a hillock, returning only a few minutes later carrying small blue eggs. "Look what I got, Jak! Do you want one?"

"Sure," Jak told him, holding out his hand.

Looking disappointed, Tobi shuffled away a few steps. "They probably aren't fresh. I wouldn't want to cause you tummy trouble, Jak. You probably shouldn't eat any."

"Then why did you offer them to me?" Jak asked, trying not to laugh.

"Because I'm an extra-considerate person!" said Tobi. "Everyone always says—"

"Shh!" said Herbert. "Listen!"

Jak glanced at the unicorn, whose ears were pricked toward the next hill. He turned toward the hill, but couldn't see anything at first. Then he heard it—a very faint, very shrill whistle like the kind he'd heard people use in the human world to call their dogs. The sound grew louder as they stood waiting for the source of the sound to appear.

Tobi shrieked and threw up his hands as a dark shadow swept over them. The eggs he'd been holding flew through the air, splattering on the ground when they hit. Pressing his hands to his ears, the little goblin ran behind Jak and tried to make himself look as small as possible.

Jak had never seen a griffin before and couldn't help but admire the way it soared over them, its eagle wings spread wide to catch the updraft from the hills. The griffin was enormous, with the lower body of a full-sized male lion and the upper body, head, and wings of a golden eagle. It eyed them as it flew past, the sound becoming a scream as it turned and banked in their direction.

"That whihtling thound cometh from the air ruthing over their lion clawth," said Lamia Lou. "Thee how he can't tuck hith back legth clothe to hith body?"

"Are you sure griffins are afraid of lamias?" Tobi asked, peeking out from behind Jak. "Because he doesn't look afraid to me."

Lamia Lou shaded her eyes with her hand and watched as the griffin drew closer. "Maybe he hathn't theen me yet." Rising up on her tail, the lamia waved her arms in the air and shouted, "Thoo! Go away!"

The griffin opened his beak and screamed. Whimpering, Tobi tried to dig a hole in the ground.

"Uh, Lamia Lou, I think Tobi's right," said Jak. "That griffin doesn't look like he's afraid of anything. Don't worry. I can handle him." He reached into his pocket and pulled out a comb. Transmogrification was one of the skills Jak had learned in goblin school. Unlike full-blooded goblins who could turn one natural object into another, he could turn one manufactured object into another. He'd found that he could make even intricate machinery, provided he'd studied an example and knew how it worked. However, right now he didn't need anything so complex.

A simple sword would work just fine. Jak held up the comb and concentrated.

Bobbing his head up and down, Herbert snorted, and pawed at the ground. "If he comes any closer, I'll get him with my horn!"

The lamia sighed. "He mutht be a young one if he doethn't know enough to be afraid of me. He needth to be taught a lethon. I'm the one who thaid we thould go thith way, tho it'th up to me to deal with that griffin. I wath jutht hoping I wouldn't have to do thith. Thtand back, everyone. I can handle thith guy."

Lamia Lou coiled her tail beneath her, waiting for the griffin's return. The beast swooped low, the eagle claws on the front of its body reaching. "Duck!" shouted Lamia Lou.

Jak threw himself to the ground when Lamia Lou shouted, and Tobi was already halfway into a hole he'd dug for himself, so the griffin veered toward the still-standing unicorn. Lamia Lou shrieked as the griffin descended on Herbert, but the unicorn was lunging and thrashing, and she couldn't get near him. Then Herbert swung his head around, smashing his horn into the griffin's foot and breaking off one of the beast's talons. Screaming, the griffin grappled with Herbert until he was able to wrap his remaining talons around the horn. He was straining to lift Herbert off the ground when Lamia Lou launched herself into the air like a suddenly released coiled spring. Latching on to the griffin's leg with her hands, she swung her tail up and over its back, getting an unbreakable hold on its massive body.

Herbert was half off the ground when Lamia Lou began to squeeze the griffin around the middle. Jak peered up as the griffin screamed. Seeing the griffin half lift, half drag Herbert, Jak jumped to his feet. Precious seconds ticked away as he refocused on the comb he was holding. He pictured what he wanted it to become—a sword made of steel with a razor-sharp blade. Suddenly the sword was in his hand, so heavy that he dropped it and had to bend down to pick it up. When he stood, the griffin had dragged Herbert nearly twenty feet.

"Let go!" shrieked Lamia Lou, her face growing red as she squeezed the griffin.

The griffin thrashed the air with his wings, sending up a cloud of dust that made everyone cough. Herbert squealed as he danced on the tips of his hooves across the ground, partly suspended under the beast that wasn't quite strong enough to lift a full-grown unicorn.

Suddenly the griffin had had enough. Opening his claws, he released Herbert's horn so that the unicorn fell to the ground with his legs sprawled under him. Without the unicorn to weigh him down, the griffin was able to fly a bit higher, though he still had an enraged lamia on his back. Twisting and turning, he tried to tear at Lamia Lou with his eagle talons and lion claws, but by now Lamia Lou had wriggled around the griffin so that her upper body was behind his head where he couldn't snap at her with his beak. She screamed as she pulled out handfuls of feathers, flinging them into the air.

"Lou!" bellowed Herbert as he got to his feet. "Let him go!"

The griffin looked as if he wanted nothing more now than to get away from the lamia. His eyes were wild as he thrashed around. Soon his breathing became labored and his wing beats slowed, and then he was plummeting from the sky and everyone below him was trying to figure out where he might land so they could get out of his way.

"Lou!" Herbert yelled. "Jump!"

Lamia Lou slithered off the griffin's back seconds before the unconscious beast hit the ground. "Oof! Ouch! Oh my!" she cried as she tumbled across the rocky terrain. When she finally stopped rolling, she lay still with only her chest moving as she struggled to catch her breath.

"Are you all right, my darling?" Herbert called as he galloped to her side.

"I'm fine," she said, sitting up. "Jutht a little bruithed ith all."

"Mmf!" came a muffled voice from where the griffin lay.

Lamia Lou turned around. "Who thaid that?"

"I think it was Tobi," said Jak. "Tobianthicus, are you under there?" Jak ran to where the griffin lay like a dead sparrow with its beak open and its eyes glazed.

"Unh!" Tobi groaned.

Lamia Lou and Herbert both had to help Jak drag the still-breathing griffin aside before they could get to Tobi. The little raccoon goblin drew in a long, shuddering breath when he was finally uncovered. Groaning, he sat up and glared accusingly at his companions. "Fine friends you are," he grumbled. "I could have suffocated, stopped breathing, lost all my air while you three fooled around."

"We're sorry, Tobi," Jak said, although he couldn't keep from grinning. "Next time we'll pay more attention to where you dig your hole." While his friends gathered around the griffin, Jak turned the sword back into a comb and shoved it into his pocket.

"What about him?" Herbert asked. He poked the griffin with his hoof and sniffed the motionless body.

Lamia Lou bent over the griffin. When she stood up again, she said, "He'll be fine. Jutht a little bit thore."

"If you don't mind my asking," said Jak, "why didn't you bite the griffin when you had the chance?"

The lamia looked shocked. "Why would I do that? I wath trying to teach him a lethon, not poithon him!"

Herbert snorted and glanced from side to side. "Which way do we go from here? A tussle like that gets me all turned around."

"Thith way," Lamia Lou said, pointing. "I'm very good at directionth. Lamiath have to be or we'd get lotht in the tall grath."

"I'm too tired, worn out, exhausted to go anywhere," Tobi whined. "That fight took a lot out of me."

Lamia Lou sighed. "Oh, all right. I'll give you a ride. You might as well climb on, too, Jak. I can move a lot fathter than you, and we've already lotht a lot of time."

"I'd offer to help, but my head hurts," said Herbert.

"That'th okay, Thweetie," Lamia Lou said, brushing his forelock out of his eyes. "You've been through a lot."

"Tobi, where are you going?" Jak asked as the little raccoon goblin scurried away.

"I want a souvenir," Tobi replied, snatching up a griffin feather and waving it in the air. "You don't come across these every day."

Lamia Lou motioned to the little goblin. "Hurry up if you want a ride. We're leaving now, with or without you. Collecting thouvenirth," she muttered, shaking her head. "The next thing you know, he'th going to want an autograph."

# Chapter 9

Once again Dasras was waiting for Tamisin when she woke. She wasn't sure how she felt about it; she was angry at him, but despite what had happened, the little voice inside her was back, and it kept insisting that she loved him. Maybe she'd responded so negatively to his kiss because she had been more tired than she'd realized. Then again, it had occurred to her that though he'd insisted that she must love him, he'd never said that he loved her. And what did he mean when he said that she *had* to love him? Did he honestly think he was that irresistible? Irinia had said that he thought he had a way with girls. Could that be what she was talking about?

Tamisin was tempted to tell Dasras to go away, but at least he wanted to spend time with her. No one else seemed interested in even talking to her, except Irinia and Malcolm, and they were busy with their own tasks.

Tamisin felt lonely, which seemed a new experience. Back at home she always had her friends or family to talk to when she needed to work something out. And there used to be that other person, the one she couldn't quite remember . . . It was a boy, she was sure of that, but not being able to picture his face or remember his name or anything about him made her feel as if she had a hole inside of her. Whoever he was, she could have talked to him about nearly anything.

A wave of homesickness washed over her. She missed her human parents, her brothers, and her friends. She missed a normal human life where she knew what to expect and—

"Tamisin!" Dasras called.

Deciding that she'd rather go with Dasras than be by herself, Tamisin slipped on her new shoes and released her wings.

"Miss me?" Dasras asked when she landed on the ground beside him. Tamisin half expected him to try to kiss her again, but instead he handed her a small bouquet of violets and began to talk about a place he wanted to show her.

That morning they visited the path lined with fairy sculptures made from living plants; her favorite was the ivy shaped into a statue of Oberon. They were on their way to lunch when they noticed a commotion on one of the paths. A group of fairies were hauling covered baskets down the path, and everyone had to step aside to let them pass. "What's that all about?" Tamisin asked Dasras.

"I don't know. What's going on?" he asked one of the passing fairies.

"Some minor trouble at the perimeter," said the warrior. "Nothing we can't handle."

"Is everything all right?" Tamisin asked Dasras as the warriors moved on.

"I'm sure it's fine," he said. "This kind of thing happens all the time." When Tamisin looked doubtful, he smiled and took her arm. "You worry too much. After lunch, we'll go to the lake where a trained sea monster is giving rides. I think you'll enjoy it."

Tamisin glanced at the fairies around them and relaxed when she saw that no else seemed concerned. Maybe this time Dasras was right. Maybe she did worry too much.

🦋

They were sitting down to eat their lunch when a fairy laughed, sounding just like Tamisin's human mother. Tamisin turned without thinking, and couldn't help but feel disappointed when she saw the group of fairies. The sound made her feel homesick again and more than a little worried. Who knew what her human parents had gone through since the night she disappeared? They had to be frantic by now. She wanted to go home, but there was no telling when she'd have the opportunity to get to know her father again. Once she went home to the human world, she'd want to stay there for a while. There was something she needed to do there—someone she needed to see.

Frowning, she rubbed her forehead, trying to ease the

headache that had started behind her eyes. Dasras must have noticed, because he studied her face for a moment, then said, "Is something wrong?"

"No. It's just that . . . well, I can't help feeling that something is wrong, or something important is missing."

Dasras nodded. "It's Titania, isn't it? Finding out that your mother lied to you would unsettle anyone."

"No, that's not it," Tamisin said. "I wasn't thinking about her at all."

"Why don't we do something to get your mind off whatever is making you look so serious? Bring your apple and you can finish it on the way to the lake. That sea monster won't be giving rides forever."

Tamisin's headache faded away as they walked through the forest. The sky was clear, and the gentle breeze that stirred the leaves on the trees was just enough to relieve the heat of the day. They could hear the crowd long before they reached the lake. Fairies filled the meadow that ran from the waterfront to the edge of the meandering path, jostling for a place in line or to watch the lucky fairies already riding on the sea monster's back.

Dasras glared at the fairies in front of them, and sounded annoyed when he said, "You shouldn't have to wait."

"I don't mind," Tamisin told him. "Look, the line is moving quickly."

It wasn't until the fairies in front of them had shuffled closer to the water that they could see the sea monster. It was long and narrow with a head like an enormous dog and a body that went up and down in humps and troughs. A nymph was perched on the monster's head, controlling it with two of the tendrils that trailed from the monster's cheeks. More than a dozen fairies sat on the humps behind the nymph, holding on to other tendrils that radiated from the monster's body.

Fairies shouted and everyone looked up. A squadron of fairy warriors was flying in formation overhead, doing loops and spirals, climbing and diving in ways that a human fighter pilot would have envied. They swung low over the sea monster, and the beast roared; all the fairies on its back clapped.

"What are they doing?" Tamisin asked.

"Practicing," Dasras told her. "The real show is on Midsummer's Eve, when it's dark and all you can see are the lights the fairies' wings make."

When the squadron left, the line in front of Tamisin and Dasras thinned out as fairies vied to take to the air and copy the maneuvers of the fairy warriors. Soon it was Tamisin and Dasras's turn to climb aboard the sea monster's back. Tamisin sat directly behind the nymph and in front of Dasras. The monster was squishy, and its dark green skin was pebbly and rough. Tendrils trailed past Tamisin's legs like smooth, wet rope. She reached down and grasped one on either side, wrapping them around her wrists for a better grip. When she looked up, she discovered that she was directly behind a large hole in the back of the monster's head. They were just starting to move when the monster whuffed and damp, fishy-smelling air blasted Tamisin in the face. She blinked and rubbed her eyes. Maybe this wasn't such a good seat after all.

Watching the sea monster from the shore, Tamisin hadn't realized how much it undulated in the water, but as soon as it began to swim, water splashed over her legs and feet. They were making their first circuit around the lake when a new group of fairies took to the air. The sea monster raised its head to look at them, and Tamisin could feel it quiver beneath her. After that the monster swam faster, as if trying to get away from the fairies.

*It's afraid!* Tamisin thought, and her heart went out to the poor beast. She glanced behind her, but no one else seemed to have noticed.

The sea monster had just started its second circuit when the flying fairies began their lowest approach. Then one of the fairies dropped something and it fell past Tamisin, landing in the hole in the back of the sea monster's head.

The monster lurched to a halt, and half the fairies tumbled off its back. All Tamisin could do was hold on to the tendrils and dig her knees into the monster's sides, but she could hear fairies shouting behind her. When the monster began thrashing from side to side, Dasras and the rest of the fairies fell off and the voices behind her stopped. Deciding that she'd be safer in the water than on the monster's back, Tamisin tried to get off, but her feet were trapped in the tendrils. She was jerking at her legs, trying to free them, when the monster tossed its head, sending the nymph who'd been trying to control it flying.

The monster swung its head around to face Tamisin and she shrank back. It snapped at the air only a yard from where she sat, and its doleful eyes looked panic stricken. And then it dove, heading straight for the bottom of the lake. Tamisin barely had time to fill her lungs before she was underwater. She was still trying to pull her legs free when the monster changed direction and headed for the surface. Its head was thrown back so far that Tamisin could see a round, white stone filling the fluttering edges of the hole. That must be what the fairies had dropped. If only she could get the stone out . . .

Tamisin reached for the stone but was thrown back when the beast began to thrash again. One of her feet came loose and she slid sideways, still held fast on the other side. She glanced down when she felt new pressure on her leg. A nymph was there, trying to unwrap the tangled tendrils that were holding Tamisin in place. Fighting the urge to draw a breath, Tamisin clung to the sea monster's back for one more agonizing moment until suddenly her leg was free and the nymph was tugging her to the surface. But there was something that Tamisin had to do first. Pulling away from the nymph, she shot out her hand, dug her fingers into the hole, grasped the stone, and ripped it from the opening. A gush of fishy air shoved her halfway to the surface.

Tamisin surfaced with a lung-wrenching gasp. Her hand was shaky as she pushed her streaming hair off her face. "Thank you," she told the nymph who had dragged her up.

"I'm glad I could help," the nymph replied. "That

whisker was tied around your foot so tight, I thought I'd never get it undone. Why did you tie yourself on, anyway?"

Tamisin was confused. "I didn't."

The nymph gave her an odd look, then flipped her head to toss her hair over her shoulder and said, "My mistake. Thanks for helping Rudie. I don't know why the fairies like dropping stones into his breathing vent, but that's not the first time it's happened." With a wave of her hand, she dove back into the water.

"Are you all right?" Dasras called to Tamisin from the shore where he and a crowd of fairies had been watching.

"I'm fine," Tamisin said, grateful when he reached out to give her a hand up.

When she was standing beside him, Dasras eyed her clothes. "You should go change. Your father sent word that he wants to talk to you."

"Did you see what happened? A fairy dropped a stone in the sea monster's breathing vent! Do you think we should tell my father?"

"What difference would it make?" asked Dasras.

"We could have drowned!"

"Fairies are always playing pranks like that. It's what they do for fun. Your father couldn't do anything unless he had proof and knew who dropped it. And even then he probably wouldn't do much. Where's the stone now?"

Tamisin shrugged. "At the bottom of the lake, I guess. I dropped it after I pulled it out."

"Then I wouldn't bother telling him," Dasras said.

"But what about the monster's tendrils or whiskers or

whatever it is you call them? Someone tied me onto the monster's back!"

Dasras frowned. "Why would anyone do that?"

"That's what I'd like to know!" said Tamisin.

"There's no way to prove that either. All I can say is that you'd better hurry. Oberon doesn't like being kept waiting."

Tamisin would have liked nothing better than to rest and gather her thoughts, but she doubted Oberon would understand if she didn't go to him as soon as she could. Dashing back to the tree where she slept, she changed into a dry dress, then hurried to Oberon's glade.

A group of fairy warriors surrounded the fairy king, looking stern faced and serious. Mountain Ash was there as well, his expression grimmer than the rest. While Oberon spoke in muted tones to the colonel, Tamisin waited at the edge of the glade. She was there only a few minutes when the fairy king glanced up and saw her.

"Ah, there she is," he said, and gestured to the fairy warriors. Although they bowed and backed away, Tamisin could feel their eyes on her as she approached the king. "I've been meaning to send for you, but other matters have demanded my attention. We never finished our conversation yesterday. Have you been enjoying yourself, my dear? Have you settled in?"

"Yes, thank you, Your Majesty."

"Please, call me Father."

Tamisin's eyes flicked to the fairies standing beside Oberon and noticed their surprise. "Are you sure it's all right? I mean, it's not as respectful as Your Majesty."

Oberon chuckled. "I would be honored if you called me Father. It's something I've wanted to hear for centuries. How are you faring? Has everyone been good to you?"

"Yes, except . . . ," she said, and hesitated, remembering what Dasras had told her.

"Go on," he said.

A tiny messenger fairy darted into the glade and hovered by Mountain Ash. The colonel tilted his head to listen and began to frown as the fairy spoke.

Tamisin wanted to tell Oberon about the incident with the sea monster, but she saw his eyes and his attention shift to the colonel and the messenger fairy and decided it wasn't the right time. "Nothing, really," she said, and was disappointed when he didn't press for her real answer. "Dasras has been showing me around."

"Good," said Oberon, still watching the colonel. "And the others? I trust my fairies are making you feel welcome."

"Yes, they are." If she'd thought she really had his attention, she would have been tempted to tell him about the cold glances and the comments she'd overheard, but she thought it would be petty and not make any difference anyway.

"Fine, fine," he said, although he was looking at Mountain Ash, not her. She glanced toward the colonel and saw the nod he gave to Oberon. The fairy king finally turned to look at Tamisin, saying, "I'm sorry, my dear. I brought you here to get to know you better, but it appears that the report I've been expecting has arrived."

"I understand," she said, although she couldn't help but feel disappointed. Tamisin backed away as she'd seen the other fairies do, embarrassed that she had simply walked away the last time she saw the king. She didn't know anything about protocol in a fairy court, so she resolved to start paying attention. It wouldn't do to embarrass her father just when their relationship was . . .

"I don't care what your spies tell you. Titania isn't about to send her army here," Oberon told Mountain Ash, his voice loud and angry. "I know my wife. When she's in the wrong, she always backs down. She deceived *me*! The last thing she's going to want to do is make me angrier."

Tamisin froze, watching Oberon's face. She wanted to hear more, but the voices grew quieter after that and she couldn't make out what anyone was saying. She'd been taught that eavesdropping was wrong, but who could blame her for listening when it was about her own mother! And what was that about her mother's army?

A thick fog began to form around the glade, making it impossible to see Oberon or anyone with him. "I guess that means he really does want me to leave," she murmured to herself, and hurried away, wishing she knew what was going on.

Tamisin's stomach rumbled. She would have loved a hamburger and french fries, but she knew that the main item on the menu was bound to be fruit, so she headed for the rock where Irinia served the food, hoping that the woman would be there and could be talked into serving something else.

Irinia and her helpers were at the far end of the rock examining a basket of fruit that a dog-goblin man was holding when Tamisin arrived. One of the fairies noticed her approach and nudged the fairy beside her. They all turned to look as Tamisin reached them, although none of them said hello. There was a flurry of movement as they each reached for one last piece of food, then moved off. Tamisin tried to ignore them.

While waiting for Irinia to come over, Tamisin glanced down at the food spread out on the rock. There was the usual fruit, of course, but there was also a platter of wafers dotted with dollops of crushed berries. She reached for one, wondering what kind of fruit was on them. It was bright red, almost a fluorescent color that she hadn't seen in fairy food before. Mashed into a seedy pulp, it smelled like raspberries, cranberries, and the extra-sweet smell of something she didn't recognize.

She had just brought the wafer to her mouth and was about to bite down when one of Irinia's faces glanced her way. The woman shrieked, lunged across the rock, and knocked the wafer from Tamisin's hand. "Don't eat that!" she cried.

"Why not?" asked Tamisin, startled.

"Because it's not fresh!" Irinia said in a loud voice, glancing at the fairies who had stopped to watch. A couple of the fairies snickered and they all moved on. While one of her faces watched the fairies, the other whispered so only Tamisin could hear, "Those have frillet berries on them. Anyone who eats them who isn't a full-blood fairy would have hallucinations, or worse. Just a few berries would be enough. I never put them out except at Oberon's request, and he didn't ask for these. Those fairies must have done this," she said, glancing at the group that was walking away. "They're probably testing you to see if you're a full-blood. Are you all right? Did you eat any?"

"No more than a tiny taste," said Tamisin.

"That shouldn't hurt you," said Irinia. "But you should probably lie down for a while. Here, rinse your mouth out with this, then drink the rest." She handed Tamisin a hollowed-out gourd filled with spring water, and watched while Tamisin swished some in her mouth, then spit it out at the base of a tree.

"I was hoping to get something to eat," said Tamisin after swallowing a sip. "Those wafers . . ."

"Here, take these," Irinia said, giving her a handful of plain ones. "Now go lie down, and be careful what you eat the next time you're hungry!"

Tamisin nodded and turned to go. It wasn't until she was halfway to the tree where she slept at night that she thought of an important question. Why, if she was supposed to be the daughter of Titania and Oberon, and therefore a full-blooded fairy, did Irinia think that the frillet berries would hurt her? Did her friend think that Tamisin was part human, or was she just being extra careful?

Tamisin took Irinia's advice and retreated to her bed to lie down. She'd never been in her hanging bed past daybreak, and it seemed odd to rest when everyone else was busy. After only a few minutes of lying on her back, staring up through the branches overhead, Tamisin thought about getting up again until she noticed that the leaves of the trees looked strange. The colors seemed to shift in a way that a change of light couldn't explain. She saw other colors like a deeper red and an odd blue that she'd never seen on leaves before. A leaf with a strong blue tinge was hanging right over her bed; when she reached out to touch it, she found it felt dry and not as supple as the rest. She wondered if the colors might actually mean something about the leaves.

A black-and-brown-banded caterpillar inched past. Tamisin had never seen anything like the pale green haze around it, although she had read about auras. A bee with a yellow haze landed on her hand, then flew away, leaving pollen-dust footprints. Tamisin was amazed that she could see something as tiny as the footprints of a bee. When it occurred to her that the odd things she was seeing might be what fairies saw every day, she began to look around with greater interest.

Eventually her lids grew heavy as she drifted off to sleep and the most colorful dreams she'd ever had.

# Chapter 10

Jak and his friends had crossed only half the length of the Griffin Hunting Grounds when the sun started to go down. "This is as good a place as any to spend the night," said Herbert, snuffling a clump of dry-looking grass.

"We could keep walking," said Jak. "The sky is clear and the moon is only a few nights away from being full."

"I'm tired," Tobi said, showing them an exaggerated yawn.

"Tho am I," said Lamia Lou. "We could all do with a good nighth retht."

Jak shrugged. He was eager to reach Tamisin, but even he knew that they would make better time the next day if they weren't dragging their feet. "It means sleeping under the open sky," he said.

"I've done it before," said Tobi.

"Yeah, but not in the Griffin Hunting Grounds," replied Jak.

"We're a long way from any shelter," said Herbert. "We'll be fine if we take turns keeping watch."

"I'll take the first watch," Jak volunteered. "I'm not tired yet." He swung his backpack off his shoulder and was looking for a place to sit when he nearly tripped over Tobi. The little goblin was curled up on the ground, already sound asleep.

"I'm not so sure we should ask him to take a turn," said Herbert.

Jak shook his head. "I think we'd all sleep better if we didn't."

Hours passed while Jak stared into the dark, but neither a griffin nor any other creature moved in the night sky. Herbert slept standing up while Lamia Lou lay stretched out beside him, her head pillowed on her arms. When it was the unicorn's turn, Jak lay on the hard ground, worrying about Tamisin. He didn't think he would sleep, but suddenly it was morning, the sky was growing lighter, and Lamia Lou was poking him and telling him it was time to get up.

Herbert was already munching grass when Jak opened his pack and took out one of the granola bars he'd brought from home. Seeing the pleading look on Tobi's face, he sighed and reached in for another. "Would you like one?" he asked Lamia Lou, but she shook her head.

"I've already eaten my breakfast," she said.

Jak didn't want to know what she'd eaten.

They spent most of that day crossing the seemingly end-less rolling hills without seeing any more griffins. By late afternoon they had reached a pine forest and Jak was relieved that he could stop watching the sky.

"Are we almost there yet?" Tobi asked for the hun-dredth time that day.

"We're thtill mileth from the Great Ditch," said Lamia Lou. "We'll thleep in the foretht tonight and reach the Ditch tomorrow. What ith it, Herbert?" she asked, glanc-ing at the unicorn, who had stopped walking.

Herbert had his head up, his mouth open, and his lips curled back to smell the air. "I smell a unicorn!"

"Gee, what a surprise," muttered Tobi. "I didn't want to mention it, but I thought you were a little whiffy."

Herbert snorted and glared at the raccoon goblin. "I don't mean me! I smell another unicorn. And there's some-thing else..." He sniffed again, then started walking, stopping every now and then to check the scent. They had reached the edge of a clearing when Herbert swung his head around, blocking Jak's way with his horn.

"What—" Jak began.

"Shh!" whispered Herbert. "Just look."

Jak peered between the leaves, trying to see. There was a unicorn, black with a white mane and tail, slowly approaching a girl with long blond hair. The girl was seated on the ground, her skirts spread out around her. She had her back to Herbert and his friends, so they couldn't see her face, but from the black unicorn's adoring expression Jak was certain that she had to be beautiful.

"This is a very special moment," Herbert whispered. "The unicorn is about to claim his maiden."

While they watched, the unicorn knelt beside the maiden, then lay down, resting his head in her lap. He gazed up at her adoringly while she caressed his forelock. Finally, he closed his eyes in contentment.

Silently the maiden inched back her skirt and slid out a halter that had been hidden under it. The unicorn still had his eyes closed when she slipped the halter on him and shoved his head off her lap. Springing to her feet, she watched as a swarm of armed goblins emerged from the trees.

"Here," the girl said, handing the biggest goblin the lead line attached to the halter. "He's all yours." Raising her hand, she snatched off the blond wig she was wearing and tossed it aside. "I hate that thing! It makes my head itch." She dug her fingers into her own short, thick hair and scratched her head with both hands at once. When she turned around, Jak saw that, like all the goblins gathered near her, she had the wide forehead and blunt ears of a wolverine goblin. Just like them, she had long, pointed teeth that looked sharp enough to bite through tanned leather.

The unicorn must have been in a daze, because it took him some time to react. When he finally tried to get to his feet, goblins piled onto his back, weighing him down.

"Hold his head still," said the goblin in charge. While some of the still-standing goblins jumped to do as he asked, the others scurried out of his way as their leader knelt beside the unicorn. Taking a hatchet off his belt, the goblin used the weapon to tap the base of the unicorn's horn as if to gauge where to hit it. He was raising the hatchet high when Herbert screamed, leaped out of the concealing brush, and charged.

The goblins shrieked and scattered before the angry white unicorn. Herbert followed the leader, rearing and striking with his front hooves, driving the goblin back into the trees. The rest of the goblins stopped at the edge of the clearing, waiting to see what their leader would do. With a wave of his arm, he gestured for them to return to the clearing and they advanced, wielding hatchets and swearing.

The moment the goblins had scrambled off his back, the black unicorn had lunged to his feet. Now he thundered to the center of the clearing and turned to face the other goblins.

After one last lunge at the goblin leader, Herbert spun around on his rear hoof and joined the black unicorn in the middle of the clearing, back to back, facing the circling goblins. The goblins darted forward to hack at necks and legs. Herbert and the black unicorn struck at them, sending some reeling while others fell to the ground until their fellow goblins dragged them away.

Stunned, Lamia Lou, Jak, and Tobi had remained in the trees, but when a goblin barely missed whacking Herbert with his hatchet, the lamia screamed, "Enough!" She slithered into the clearing, fangs bared, hissing loudly.

The goblins saw her; they froze for a moment, then fled the clearing, screaming.

Jak hurried to make sure that Herbert and the black unicorn were uninjured. As the last goblin disappeared from sight, Tobi dropped out of the tree he'd climbed and followed Jak.

"Don't worry about me," Herbert was telling Lamia Lou when Jak arrived. "They didn't even get close."

"You are tho wonderful!" Lamia Lou told him with shining eyes. "I've never met anyone braver!"

"I have to thank you," said the black unicorn, who had trotted to the edge of the clearing to make sure that the goblins were really gone. "I would have been in a real fix if you hadn't . . . Whoa! Who is this lovely lady?"

The unicorn was ogling Lamia Lou in a way that Herbert obviously didn't like. He snorted and lowered his horn at the other unicorn, stepping closer so that his rival had to back away. "This lovely lady is mine!" Herbert said. "Take one step toward her and I'll skewer you where you stand."

"Easy, boy, easy!" said the black unicorn, although he didn't take his eyes off Lamia Lou. "You can't blame a fellow for being interested."

"You might want to try being a little more careful about the maiden you choose," said Jak.

"Don't I know it!" the black unicorn exclaimed. "I thought there was something off when I sniffed that girl, but there's a shortage of maidens around, so I can't afford to be too choosy. As for *this* lovely—"

"I told you to back off!" said Herbert.

"Sorry! I'd heard that the goblins started poaching uni-corn horns the minute Titania sent her army to fight Oberon, but I didn't expect to come across them so soon. However, if I'd known that getting tackled by a gang of goblins meant that I'd get to meet this lovely lady, I'd have—"

"All right, it's time for us to go," Herbert announced. Nudging Lamia Lou with his nose, he stepped between her and the black unicorn. "It was nice meeting you, but I have to tell you—stay away from my lady or our next meeting won't be so friendly."

"I understand," said the black unicorn. "But if you two ever break up—"

Lamia Lou didn't look back as Herbert herded her from the clearing, but Jak did, and he noticed that Herbert did as well. The black unicorn must have seen them, because he put on a mournful expression that made Herbert snort and walk faster.

They hadn't gone far before the sun started to set. When Lamia Lou assured them that they still had miles to go, they began to look for a good place to sleep. It was Tobi who finally found a likely tree, and after eating some of the provisions that the lamias had packed for them, Jak and the raccoon goblin climbed into the branches and settled down for the night. Herbert had offered to stand guard first, so Lamia Lou curled up around a branch above his head on the other side of the tree. Jak couldn't see them, but he could just make out the glint of Tobi's eyes only a few branches away.

"Jak," Tobi whispered. "One of my informants told me something about you and Tamisin. He said that you two aren't getting along so well anymore."

Jak sighed. Of course Tobi had heard about it. Titania's fairies had seen it for themselves and were probably telling everyone. "It's true," said Jak. "Everything was great when we first went back to the human world, but then things started to fall apart."

"Did you forget her name or complain that she'd poisoned you with her cooking? That makes a girl real mad, especially if you do it when her whole family is there for dinner."

"It wasn't anything like that," said Jak. "Tamisin wanted to come back to the land of the fey and got mad at me when I didn't tell her that the gate behind my house was open. I would have told her, but it never occurred to me that she could go through cat-goblin territory. It wasn't somewhere I would have gone, so I didn't think it was safe for her, either. She kept trying to go through the gate behind our school. You know the one—it opens into Titania's forest. It was always closed, though, but because Titania had placed a compulsion on her . . ."

A snuffling snort from Tobi's branch made Jak raise his head to look at his friend. The little goblin was asleep, lying on his back with his mouth open. Jak wondered how long he'd been talking to himself.

He turned over, trying to get comfortable on the branch. He could hear Lamia Lou and Herbert talking in lowered voices. When he closed his eyes, he pictured Tamisin's face, and wondered if she ever thought about him. He didn't fall asleep until all of his companions were quiet and he had himself half convinced that Tamisin probably missed him as much as he missed her.

# Chapter 11

It was morning when Tamisin woke to the sound of Dasras's voice. She was disappointed to see that everything looked normal once again. Sighing, she leaned over the edge and said, "I'll be right there."

"I thought you might like to go for a walk," he said.

"I'd love to," Tamisin replied. When she landed beside him, he reached for her hand, but she didn't take it. It wasn't that she didn't like holding hands, just that she was uncomfortable holding his.

"How was your visit with your father?" asked Dasras as they walked down the path.

"Fine," she said with a shrug. "Although it was very short. He was more interested in something else than in me."

"You can't blame him for that," said Dasras. "He's a great king and he takes his rule seriously. It was good of him to make time to see you at all."

Tamisin was surprised at the vehemence in his voice. "You really like him, don't you?"

Dasras glanced at her, then looked away. "He's the closest I've ever come to having a father. You should be happy that he's yours."

Tamisin was about to reply, but they had already reached the rock where Irinia and the nymphs were serving fruit and a fruit-flavored drink. Stepping away from Dasras, Tamisin included the nymphs in the friendly look she gave Irinia, then said to the two-faced woman, "Thank you for your suggestion. I'm glad I listened to you."

"You're welcome," said Irinia.

The nymphs' expressions softened, as if all it took were a few friendly words. Tamisin would have liked to stay and talk to them, but Dasras bumped her with his arm, gave her a pointed look, and handed her a peach. She was letting him herd her away when a voice behind them said in a loud whisper, "She's nice! Are you sure she's a fairy?"

"I've seen her wings," someone replied.

Dasras scowled and glanced back over his shoulder. "It isn't their place to talk about you like that."

Tamisin laughed. "Why not? The fairies do. You heard Lily and Hawthorne the other day."

"That's different," said Dasras.

"How is it different?"

Dasras stopped where he was and swung around to face her. "It just is! Fairies are better than everyone else, and everyone knows it! Do you think Lily would have ordered another fairy to deliver her flowers to an ogress?

Not in a million years! But I'm not a fairy, and even though Oberon treats me better than most, everyone knows that he does it on a whim. When he changes his mind, I'll be sent to live on the other side of the briars and made to work like *them*," he said, jerking his head at the group behind them.

"If it's so awful, why do you stay?"

"Because I have nowhere else to go," he said, suddenly looking deflated. "I've lived in one fairy court or the other since the day I was born. It's the only life I've ever known. Look, there's one of Oberon's messengers." A tiny fairy was flying their way, zipping over and around branches and other fairies. "Oberon must want me again. Not that I contribute anything useful to our conversations, but he likes to use me as a sounding board when he has something to mull over. There's no telling how long I'll be gone. You might as well go for a walk without me."

Tamisin opened her mouth to reply, but he was already walking away. Aside from the feeling that she was supposed to love him, shouldn't she feel something more when he was around?

Feeling lost, Tamisin started down the path. As she walked, she saw flower fairies using their magic to freshen wilting flowers and straighten crooked stems. Others were directing plants to grow around obstacles to reach the little bit of sun filtering through the overhead leaves.

She was rounding a curve in the path when she came upon a group of human-sized fairies standing in a circle, watching something on the ground. Someone swore and someone else growled. A fairy moved to the side, and suddenly Tamisin could see two male ogres, rolling on the ground, wrestling. They looked much like very big men with broad, coarse features and thick, heavy builds. When one opened his mouth to snarl at the other, she saw that he had sharp, pointed teeth like a wolf's. Blood trickled from a cut running across the blond ogre's forehead. Raw-looking patches on the other's head showed where his opponent had pulled out clumps of gray-streaked brown hair. They grunted as they fought, seemingly oblivious to the crowd of fairies surrounding them.

Something soft brushed Tamisin's cheek and she turned her head. A messenger fairy was hovering beside her. The air sparkled, and a full-sized male fairy dressed all in lavender handed her a purse woven from an odd, dark green plant. "Here, Princess. This is for you," he said. "The mermaids sent it." Then the fairy shrank and flew away before Tamisin could ask any questions.

Tamisin slipped into the sheltering trees to open the purse. She gasped when a necklace tumbled into her hand. Made of enormous pearls and large coral beads, it was the prettiest piece of jewelry she'd ever held.

"Oh!" she cried. "This is gorgeous! And Dasras said the mermaids weren't nice!"

Tamisin wanted to thank the mermaids, but climbing to the top of the rocks was harder than she remembered. Finally she was standing on the beach looking out to sea and listening to the water hiss as it ran up the clean white sand. Taking off her shoes, she stepped into the advancing foam. The cool water felt good on her feet, so she began to walk along the curving beach while searching the waves for some sign of mermaids. When she nearly tripped over a large stack of seashells at the water's edge, she knew that someone had been there. A little farther on she found a pool cut off from the rest of the water, and saw a crab scuttling across the bottom. Taking a seat beside the pool, she was bending over to see what else lived there when she heard splashing and a voice called, "Hello!"

Tamisin looked up. A young woman was bobbing in the water just past the point where the waves broke. She waved, and suddenly something angled and dripping rose out of the water behind her. Tamisin was about to shout a warning when she realized that the object was a tail and it belonged to the girl.

"I'll be right there!" the mermaid called, and dove into the water with a flip of her tail.

Tamisin watched as a blue-green shape streaked just below the breaking waves. When the mermaid reached the shallows, a tongue of water rose up, carrying her above the grating pebbles at the water's edge onto the beach itself, depositing her only feet from where Tamisin was standing. Her hair, which had looked black from a distance, now looked like the deepest green. Her eyes were green as well, but a lighter shade that spoke of seaweed and kelp.

The mermaid flipped her wet hair over her shoulder

and smiled. Tamisin held up the necklace. "Are you the mermaid who sent me this?" she asked.

"I am if you're the princess, Tamisin."

"I am," said Tamisin.

"And I'm Kryllus. My friends and I just wanted to welcome you to our part of the world." The mermaid gestured toward the deep water where two more heads were bobbing.

"That's very kind of you," said Tamisin. "The necklace is lovely. Did you get the pearls around here?"

"About a hundred miles east of here, actually," said Kryllus. "Would you like to see the spot? I can take you there if you're interested. I'm a fast swimmer. It wouldn't take too long."

"I'm not sure . . . ," Tamisin began. Even though she could swim, she wasn't sure she should go into deep water with a mermaid she'd just met.

Kryllus sighed. "It would be a real shame if you didn't go. I could show you some very pretty places that you'd never get to see from the land. However, if you're afraid of the water . . ."

"I'm not afraid!" said Tamisin.

"Or would rather not socialize with mermaids like us, I'll understand."

"It isn't that! It's just . . . Never mind. I'd love to see where you found the pearls."

Kryllus clapped her hands. "That's wonderful! We'll have so much fun! I can't wait to introduce you to my friends."

"Maybe I should tell someone before we . . . ," Tamisin began.

The water rose up, lapping around her knees, rising until it was high enough to lift her off her feet. Kryllus chuckled at the expression on Tamisin's face as the water carried them past the shallows to the drop-off where the other mermaids waited. Suddenly Tamisin was left treading water, face-to-face with three mermaids.

"These are my friends, Squall and Pacifica."

The mermaid named Squall pushed her dripping silver hair off her forehead and gave Tamisin an intent look through startlingly silver eyes. When Tamisin said, "Hello," the mermaid just nodded and looked away.

The other mermaid, Pacifica, had seashell combs holding her dark blue hair back from her face. Her blue eyes sparkled when she looked at Tamisin and said, "Hi!"

"Wrap your arms around my neck and I'll carry you," said Kryllus.

Tamisin shook her head. "Oh, I couldn't. I don't want to hurt you."

"That's funny!" Kryllus said, and giggled. "You won't hurt me! Mermaids are as strong as porpoises and . . . Oh, sorry, Squall."

The silver-haired mermaid looked distressed now; Tamisin thought she saw tears in her eyes.

"Don't worry," said Pacifica, patting Squall's back. "Everything will be all right."

"Just grab hold, will you?" Kryllus told Tamisin. "She'll be fine once we start moving."

Kryllus turned around and Tamisin swam up behind her, wrapping her arms around the mermaid's neck. With one powerful thrust of her tail, the mermaid took off.

Tamisin's hands slipped and she had to fight to stay on. "Slow down!" she yelled, clutching wildly at the mermaid.

Kryllus slowed long enough for Tamisin to tighten her grip, and then they were off again, racing to deeper water, cutting across the swells so that they hit them with a *whump! whump!* Feeling the mermaid's tail undulating just below her own legs, Tamisin fought to keep her body and legs as high in the water as possible. Water smacked her in the face every time she looked up, so she kept her head down, making it difficult to see anything but Kryllus's back and long, streaming hair.

The three mermaids turned to swim side by side, moving parallel to the shore. Kryllus angled along the tops of the swells now, and Tamisin was finally able to look around. On one side the blue water stretched all the way to the horizon, where it met the sky in a long, straight line. The shoreline lay on the other side, close enough that Tamisin could see the land change from beach to rocks to cliff.

Even as they shot through the waves, Kryllus tried to tell Tamisin what they were passing. "The griffins sun themselves on those rocks," she shouted at one point. "That's the River Spleen where ogre captains come down to the sea in their ships," she shouted a short time later.

Tamisin opened her mouth to speak, and got a mouthful of salt water. She turned her head to spit it out before asking, "The ogres have ships?"

The mermaid nodded. "A long time ago, they used them for raiding expeditions, but ever since Titania and Oberon conquered all the fey, the ogres have taken up more honest pursuits. Now the captains act as middlemen between the farmers and miners and the ones who buy their goods."

The river ran across level ground and emptied into the ocean in a wide, spreading delta. A sailing ship was returning upriver, its cargo piled on an enormous dock attached to a huge wooden building. Ogres clambered over the dock and the ships tied up alongside, carrying cargo from one to the other. Tamisin was glad the mermaids didn't try to go any closer, especially after she saw curved fins heading toward the shallower water. She'd seen enough television specials on sharks to recognize them, and had no desire to learn how mermaids and sharks got along.

After a time, Kryllus passed a long stretch of white sand beach. Patches of fog drifted over the sand, obscuring some spots while leaving others clear. Kryllus had begun to angle toward the beach when another of the sharp, piercing sounds made the mermaid turn her head. Opening her mouth, she replied with an identical sound. The other mermaids drew closer as they began to argue in shrieks and whistles, gesturing wildly as their expressions ranged from fear to sorrow to vehemence. When it was over, Kryllus shrugged and turned away from the beach to swim along the shoreline again while Squall and Pacifica raced ahead.

"What was that all about?" Tamisin asked.

"Squall and her twin sister, Tempest, grew up with a pod of porpoises. One of the porpoises is trapped on a beach near here. Tempest is taking care of him, but she just contacted Squall. Apparently the porpoise isn't doing well, so Squall wants to go straight there."

"The poor thing!" exclaimed Tamisin. "We should all be there helping him!"

Kryllus turned her head and gave Tamisin a curious look. "You're an odd one, aren't you? Fairies don't usually care about helping anyone."

"I've been noticing that I'm not like most fairies," Tamisin replied. "How far away did you say this beach was?"

"Not too far," Kryllus told her, and began to pick up speed.

They were going fast now, and the water hitting Tamisin hurt her face. Closing her eyes, she tucked her head down so that it was behind Kryllus. When she looked up again, the mermaid had turned toward an ordinary-looking beach where Squall, Pacifica, and another mermaid were already sitting well back from the water's edge.

"Hold on," said Kryllus as the water carried them to shore. When they landed next to Squall, the little bit of their wave fell to the sand in a cascade of droplets. Squall turned toward them, her long face looking even more mournful than before. Just past the mermaids, a porpoise rested in a pool of water, watching them with dark, limpid eyes.

"What's *she* doing here?" asked the mermaid who looked very much like Squall but with black hair.

"This is Tempest," Pacifica said to Tamisin. "Tempest, the princess is our guest and we must be polite."

"Why?" the mermaid snapped. "We don't need nosybodies coming around to see Swift die."

"He's not going to die!" wailed Squall, who threw herself into the pool so she could wrap her arms around the porpoise.

Tamisin knelt beside the pool. "How did he get trapped so far from the water?" She turned toward the mermaids in time to see Kryllus and Pacifica exchange a look.

"We don't know," said Tempest. "We found him like this a few hours ago."

"We can get water to him, but we can't get him out," Pacifica said.

Tamisin glanced at Kryllus. "Have you tried carrying him out to sea the way you carried me? That trick you did with the water should do it."

"That was the first thing we did," said the mermaid.

"If you all tried it together . . ."

"We did!" declared Tempest. "But we weren't strong enough. The water was just a drizzle by the time we got it this far."

Tamisin nodded. "Then what you need is more water."

"And how do you suggest we get it, Miss Know-It-All—haul it here in seashells?" said Tempest. "We need a *lot* of water to get him back in the ocean our way." The mermaid was so upset that she was shaking and bright spots of pink had appeared on her pale cheeks.

"Actually, I was thinking about a storm," Tamisin said, getting to her feet. Although she had called up storms involuntarily more than once, the only time she'd been able to do it when she wanted to had been when she was in real danger. It seemed worth a try.

Closing her eyes, Tamisin pictured a storm. She imagined roiling clouds and booming thunder and bolts of lightning heralding a deluge that would fill the little pool where the porpoise lay and wash him back out to sea. A shadow passed overhead and Tamisin looked up. The high, puffy clouds were lower now and getting thicker.

"What does she think she's doing?" Tempest said in a surly voice.

"Give her a minute," said Pacifica. "She's said to be Titania's daughter."

"And that's supposed to mean something?" said Tempest.

"Leave her alone, Tempest," Kryllus told her. "At least the fairy's trying."

"Please do something!" pleaded Squall.

Tamisin closed her eyes again. She thought about black clouds and thunder shaking the air while rain lashed the ground below.

"Would you look at that!" said Pacifica.

Tamisin opened her eyes and held up her hand. A light breeze was actually stirring the sand. Dark clouds hung overhead, and a few fat drops plopped onto her palm. She shook her head. At this rate they would all die of old age before there was enough water to move the porpoise. The only time this had worked, the storm had come hard and fast. It had been during a battle between fairies and goblins, when her own life had been at risk. She thought about how she'd felt during the battle when she wanted the storm to come—how she'd been frightened and angry, the sense of urgency . . . Storms came when she was angry, there was no way around it. If she wanted a storm now, she'd have to get mad at someone or something.

The few clouds were dissipating when Tamisin opened her eyes and tilted her face toward the sky. She thought about the trapped porpoise and the frantic mermaids. She thought about how she'd feel if someone she loved was in danger. And then she remembered when someone she loved *had* been in danger. She had gone to rescue him from a cave and together they had flown out and . . .

It was right there at the edge of her mind. She did love someone, and it wasn't Dasras. It was someone back home in the human world. Someone who loved her, too. He was the one whose name she couldn't remember, whose face she couldn't quite picture. Now Tamisin was mad at whoever had taken her memories from her.

Dark clouds scudded overhead as thunder rumbled and rain began to pelt her face and clothes. She *had* to get that life back! The air around her seemed to crackle, and she felt a tingling the length of her body, rippling along her arms and legs until her fingers and toes felt as if they were on fire. Squall squealed with delight when the rain became a deluge, just as Tamisin had pictured it. Tamisin willed the wind to grow stronger and it did, driving the rain before it so that the water engulfed the porpoise and lifted him from the pool, hurling him toward the ocean, where he plunged into the waves with a slap of his tail.

As the electric feeling coursed through her, Tamisin grew tense and the sensation seemed to build until it was almost painful. She twitched her fingers, and electricity crackled off the tips. Trying to ease the discomfort, she relaxed her muscles and was surprised when the tingling seemed to dribble from her fingers and toes. When she felt normal again, she glanced down at her hands, then up at the sky. The storm was over. The clouds had thinned, the wind calmed to a gentle breeze, and the rain turned to mist. In less than a minute the storm was gone and the only evidence of Tamisin's efforts was the storm-wracked beach, the stunned looks on the mermaids' faces, and Tamisin's knowledge that someone had tampered with her memory and her life.

"That was amazing!" breathed Squall. "I didn't know fairies could do that!"

"Most of them can't," said Kryllus, giving Tamisin an appraising look.

Tempest leaned forward to slap Tamisin on the back. "Thank you. I'm sorry I doubted you before, but you're the first fairy who's actually done something good for us. They usually act superior and make fun of mermaids."

"I can't imagine why," said Tamisin as the water began

carrying them back to the ocean. "Where I come from, mermaids are considered exotic and exciting. Some people spend their entire lives wishing they could get even the tiniest glimpse of a mermaid."

"Really? I thought you lived with Titania," said Kryllus. "I know she doesn't live anywhere near the ocean, but still . . ."

Tamisin shook her head as the water gently deposited her in the top of a swell. "Titania is my mother, but I only just met her. I grew up in the human world."

"Really?" said Squall. "I'd love to go there!"

Tempest gave her sister an exasperated glance before turning back to Tamisin. "So how did you end up at Oberon's court?"

"My father had me brought here," Tamisin told her, then thought about what she'd said. Something didn't feel quite right, although she couldn't say what.

"Where do you want to go now?" asked Pacifica. "We can take you to see those pearls in the oyster bed. It's just a little farther south."

"No, thanks," said Tamisin. She'd begun to feel a chill in the air, and noticed that the sun was lower in the sky. "I think it's time I get back to the beach where you found me."

"Then let me take you," said Tempest.

"No!" Squall said. "I get to do it!"

"We could all take turns," suggested Pacifica.

"Forget it!" said Kryllus as she swam to where Tamisin was treading water. "It's my job."

The other mermaids glowered at Kryllus as Tamisin wrapped her arms around the mermaid's shoulders.

Squall pouted for a moment, then announced, "Well, I'm going to check on Swift. I'll see you around, Tamisin!"

"I'm going, too," Tempest said with a wave of her hand, and the two sisters swam off.

Pacifica sighed. "I might as well go, since you don't need me." She gave Kryllus a hopeful look, but when her friend didn't disagree, she swam away.

"I thought they'd never leave," Kryllus said, and with a swish of her tail, started swimming west along the shoreline. They traveled in silence for a few minutes before the mermaid began to angle closer to the shore. "There's something I wanted to tell you, but I couldn't before," she said over her shoulder. "Do you see that beach?"

The fog-shrouded beach lay just ahead. As Tamisin watched, a man and a woman appeared out of the fog. Their faces were sad and oddly familiar, yet somehow Tamisin was certain that she'd never met them. Then the fog swirled again and they were gone.

"What about it?" Tamisin asked.

"That white sand is the sand of time. You set foot on that beach and time no longer has any meaning for you. It doesn't actually stand still, but it passes so slowly that it might as well. I was supposed to bring you to that beach and leave you there."

"Why?" Tamisin asked.

"A fairy messenger brought me a note this morning. It said that a dolphin was stranded on a certain beach, and if we did as the author of the note said, he would free the dolphin before midnight tonight. If we didn't do what he wanted, the dolphin would stay there until it died. Pacifica was with me when I got the note, so the two of us told Squall and Tempest, and they helped us find the dolphin. He was a good friend of theirs, which made it worse."

Tamisin was incredulous. "And the author of the note wanted you to leave me on the sands of time?"

"That's right," said Kryllus. "I'm sorry, but I didn't know what else to do. Whoever wrote the note had me send you the necklace so you'd come to the beach."

"And you don't know who wrote it?"

"I have no idea," Kryllus said, shaking her head.

"I suppose we could ask the messenger," said Tamisin. "Do you remember who brought the note?"

"Are you kidding?" said Kryllus. "There are more than a hundred fairy messengers, and they all look alike to me. I wouldn't recognize that one if he bit me on the nose."

"What should I do?" Tamisin said, mostly to herself, although she already knew the answer. Oberon's forest was no longer safe for her, and her mind felt clearer than it had in days. Someone had made her think she loved Dasras, and blocked her memories—memories that were starting to come back. It was time that she went home.

"If I were you, I'd watch my back," said the mermaid. "Somebody at Oberon's court really doesn't like you."

# Chapter 12

They arrived at the Great Ditch a few hours after dawn. "We're supposed to climb down this?" Jak said, peering over the edge of a sheer cliff. It was a lot bigger than he'd expected.

Lamia Lou nodded. "You have to if you want to get to the other thide. There'th a path over there you can uthe."

Jak eyed the path. It was only a foot or so wide in places, but he'd climbed worse. "I think I can handle it. Thanks for helping us get this far."

"I'm glad we could help," said Lamia Lou. "Thay hello to Tamithin for uth and come vithit ath thoon ath you can."

"We should head back now," Herbert told Lamia Lou. "If we hurry, we can reach the Sograssy Sea by dinnertime tomorrow."

Lamia Lou laughed and patted his back. "Thometimeth I think you love me for my tathty grath."

"You know that's not true, Sweet Lips!" said Herbert.

"Let's get out of here before they get all mushy," said Tobi, shuffling to the edge.

After thanking his friends once more and saying good-bye, Jak started down the narrow trail. Tobi had already hurried ahead, scrambling past the parts where the trail got narrower or disappeared altogether while Jak climbed down the cliff using small cracks in the rock.

"There you are, Jak boy!" chirped Tobi an hour later. "That was fun! Say, did I ever tell you what a good swimmer I am? I bet I can beat you to the other side, just like I beat you coming down. What should we bet? How about if I get across first, you carry me on your back when I get tired?"

"No bets, Tobi. I don't care who gets across first, as long as we get across. That water looks awfully fast."

Jak had gone swimming only a few times in his life, but Tobi didn't seem to be the least bit afraid, and plunged in without waiting. Unsure of how deep the river might be, Jak took a tentative step off the bank and was immediately yanked off his feet. He flopped onto his back, coming up a moment later spitting silt-flavored water and wishing he'd thought to transmogrify something into a boat. Although Jak tried to aim for the other side of the river, the current was too strong and he was dragged downstream, his arms flailing and his legs kicking wildly. He watched helplessly as the river carried his backpack and provisions out of sight. Then Tobi was splashing toward him, swimming circles around Jak and chortling in his face. Before Jak knew it, the little goblin had shoved him onto a floating log and hauled him to shore.

"I won! I won!" the raccoon goblin cried, hopping up and down. "This is the first time I've ever won anything!"

Jak groaned and tried to pull his body onto the shore. The river was still trying to drag him downstream, and he was exhausted as he finally worked his legs onto dry land. "You didn't win anything," Jak croaked, coughing up water. "I never accepted your bet."

"Don't try to get out of it now, Jak, my friend," said Tobi, rubbing his hands together. "Don't worry, I won't make you carry me up the cliff, although . . ."

"Forget it," Jak said as he heaved himself upright, water sluicing off his hair and clothes. "Thanks for helping me, but I . . ." He sighed and shook his head. The raccoon goblin had saved his life. "All right, I'll carry you, but not until we're on level ground."

"Sounds good to me! Now, which path do you think we should take? I like this one!" The little goblin disappeared up the faint hint of a trail, chuckling to himself.

Jak shivered in the shade of the rock wall as he climbed. His sodden clothes clung to him, his wet shoes made footholds slippery, and he had to force his numb fingers to work. When he finally reached the top, he flung himself down on the dusty ground, exhausted and eager to soak up the sun's warmth.

"There you are, Jak! What took you so long?" asked Tobi. "Why are you lying there like that? Time's a-wasting! We'd better get moving."

"*Now* you're in a hurry," grumbled Jak, covering his eyes with his arm. "I'll get up in a minute. You have no idea how tired I am. All I need is a little rest . . ."

"Jak, I think something's coming. It sounds pretty big, and I . . ." Tobi's voice faded off to silence, but Jak was only half awake and didn't notice.

The ground shook under Jak. He made a waving motion with his free hand and grumbled, "Leave me alone, Tobi. I said I'd get up in a minute."

"What is it, Doreen?" said a deep, rumbling voice. "Is it human? Poke it and see what it does."

"I'm not going to poke it, Curtis," replied a softer voice. "I don't think it's human anyway. Look at the shape of its face and those cheekbones . . . I think it might be a cat goblin."

Jak grunted and rolled onto his side. He was having the oddest dream, yet it seemed so real. The strange timbre of the voices, the brush of warm fur against the back of his arm . . . Jak's eyes flew open, and he sat up so suddenly that his forehead smacked the nose of the stranger bending over him.

Jak rubbed his forehead. His eyes grew wide when the stranger patted her now-bleeding nose with a lion's paw. She was a sphinx, one of the monsters that inhabited the desert, and, with the head of a human and the body of a lion, it was a creature that most people tried to avoid.

"Ow!" the sphinx exclaimed, giving Jak a reproachful glance with long-lashed eyes the color of the sky. "That hurt."

"Sorry," said Jak. "You surprised me."

"What happened, Doreen?" growled the sphinx with the deep voice. Jak shrank back when he saw the craggy face of an older man with a ruff of lion fur. "Did the goblin bite you? Let me at it!"

"Calm down, Curtis! He didn't bite me. I just bumped my nose, that's all. I have to apologize," Doreen said, turning to Jak. "He fell off a cliff this morning and hurt his shoulder. He's not usually this grumpy."

*Thunk!* A small stone hit the ground beside Jak, raising a puff of dust. He jumped to his feet and spun around. Another stone whizzed past him and hit Curtis. "Hey!" the sphinx roared. "Who threw that?"

A small figure popped up from behind a low hill and hurled another stone at the sphinxes. Jak seemed to be the only one who saw Tobi. Doreen yowled when the stone hit her.

"Stop it, Tobi!" Jak yelled.

"Run, Jak! I'll hold them off while you get away!" shouted the raccoon goblin.

Doreen whimpered as she tried to lick the spot where the rock had hit her. Curtis frowned and shook his massive head. "No one hurts my mate without answering to me!" he roared. The sphinx bounded forward, but his leg went out from under him and he crumpled to the ground.

"I'll take care of this!" said Jak, and launched himself toward the hill.

He had nearly reached the boulder that Tobi was

hiding behind when the goblin stood up again, a rock ready in his hand. Seeing his friend, Tobi shouted, "Run, scoot, skedaddle, Jak!"

"Stop throwing rocks!" Jak shouted. "You're just making them mad!"

Tobi was looking behind Jak when the little goblin's eyes suddenly went wide and he turned and darted away. Jak glanced over his shoulder. Doreen was running toward them in great ground-eating bounds with her eyes narrowed and a snarl on her lips. He turned to run away himself, but before he'd moved, she'd passed him.

"Please don't hurt him, Doreen!" Jak yelled after her even as he tried to catch up. "He thought he was helping me!"

Jak had never seen Tobi run so fast. The goblin scampered across the uneven terrain as if it were flat. He soon reached a plain covered with low-growing grass.

Doreen stopped before the grass began and sat down on her haunches. "I wouldn't go there if I were you!" she called after Tobi, who had crossed onto the grassy plain.

Jak caught up with her a moment later and ran past her after his friend. "Stop!" Doreen shouted. He kept going, but a moment later the sphinx tackled him, knocking him to the ground so that he sprawled at the edge of the grass. "But Tobi . . . ," he spluttered.

"Just ran into the Land of Forgetfulness," said Doreen, pinning him down with a paw. "You can't follow him there. If you do, you'll both be lost. I like you, young goblin, so I had to knock you down. You remind me of my youngest cub, and I'd want someone to knock him down if he was about to do something foolish."

"Tobi! Come back!" Jak yelled as loud as he could. When the little goblin kept running, Jak struggled to get free of the sphinx. "He's my friend! I have to stop him!"

"Don't you understand?" Doreen asked. "You go into the Land of Forgetfulness and you'll lose your memory. You won't remember why you're there, and you'll wander around aimlessly until you starve or something else that's lost in there eats you."

Jak stopped struggling. Doreen was right; he couldn't go in there, at least not now. He said, "I don't have time to waste. I have to get to Oberon's forest as fast as I can. Do you think Tobi'll be all right until I can come back to get him?"

They both looked to where the goblin was scampering across the grass. Jak realized that Tobi was no longer running away when his friend flopped down on the ground and began to roll over, then stopped and kicked his feet in the air. "He's playing!" Jak said in surprise.

"It looks as if he's already forgotten why he's there," said Doreen as she took her paw off Jak. "He should be fine for a while. He's a fast runner and can probably get away from most predators. I wouldn't leave him there for long, though."

"I won't," Jak said, getting to his feet.

They walked together back to where Curtis was lying on his side, licking his injured shoulder. Jak crouched down beside him and took a good look at the injury; it reminded him of something he'd seen before. "I think Curtis pulled it out of the socket," Jak said, glancing up at Doreen. "I once saw a cat goblin who did the same thing. My uncle fixed it by pulling it straight."

Doreen drew in a quick breath and glanced from Jak to her mate. "Do you think you could help Curtis?"

Jak nodded slowly. "Maybe, but it's going to hurt, so he's going to have to promise not to snap at me or anything."

"Oh, he'll promise," Doreen declared. "Won't you, Curtis?"

"I'll do anything if you can make this pain go away," groaned the male sphinx.

"Hold him down, will you?" Jak asked.

"Gladly," replied Doreen, and sat on her mate.

Curtis lay his head on the ground while Jak took hold of his paw. Digging his feet into the rocky soil, Jak leaned back and pulled. Curtis's head snapped around and his lips curled back when he snarled. Jak tugged with all his strength until he felt the shoulder pop back into place.

Curtis shuddered. Turning his head to whuff at his mate, he said, "You can get off me now."

"Are you all right, Curtis?" asked Doreen as she stood up.

Her mate clambered to his feet and shook himself. "Much better," he said, testing his weight on his shoulder. "Thank you, young goblin. You are a cat goblin, aren't you?"

"Yes, I am," Jak replied. It didn't seem the right time to explain that he was also half human.

The sphinxes were taller than he was, and Curtis's

muscles were particularly impressive, though now that he was no longer in pain, he looked friendly and kind. Glancing at Doreen, Jak smiled. He thought that their faces could have been those of a middle-aged couple in the human world and was surprised by how comfortable he felt around them.

"He reminds me of our Tomi," Doreen told Curtis, then turned to Jak and said, "Tomi is our youngest. You never met a nicer sphinx."

Curtis tilted his head to the side and studied Jak. "I see what you mean, Doreen. There is a resemblance. Not to be rude," Curtis said to Jak, "but what exactly are you doing here? We don't get many visitors, cat goblin or not."

"He said he's going to Oberon's forest," explained Doreen.

Jak nodded. "Is it very far from here?"

"It can be," said Doreen. "Unless of course you know where you're going."

"What my mate means," Curtis told him, "is that it would be easy to get lost on the way unless one had a guide. We can show you if you'd like. We don't have any more pressing engagements today, do we, Doreen?"

"Not at all," she said, smiling brightly.

The sphinxes took up position on either side of Jak as they walked. "So," said Curtis. "What happened to the rock thrower?"

"He ran into the Land of Forgetfulness," said Doreen.

"He didn't really mean any harm," Jak told them. "He's my friend Tobi, and he was just trying to help me."

Curtis chuckled. "He probably thought we were going to eat you."

"Most people are afraid of us," Doreen explained to Jak. "Although *you* don't seem to be."

"What can I say?" said Jak. "You're part big cat and I'm part cat goblin. I almost feel as if we're related."

"So do I!" Doreen said.

"I am worried about Tobi, though," said Jak. "Will he remember things once he leaves the Land of Forgetfulness?"

"After a while," Curtis told him. "A few creatures have wandered out of the Land in our direction. Some sphinxes would take advantage of their memory lapses and eat them, but Doreen and I try to help them when we can. It takes some a couple of hours, others nearly an entire day before they remember much of anything. Everyone is different."

Jak nodded. "I'd like to get Tobi out as soon as I can, but I don't have much time. Is there any way to walk through the Land of Forgetfulness without losing your memory?"

"Not as far as I know," said Curtis.

"I've heard that you'll be all right if you write yourself notes, reminding yourself why you're there," Jak told him.

Curtis chuckled. "That may be true, but then you'd have to be able to write, wouldn't you? I've never mastered that feat," he said, flexing one of his front paws.

"If you don't mind my asking, why are you going to Oberon's court?" asked Doreen.

"Someone I care about very much was kidnapped and taken there," said Jak. "I have to get her out before something bad happens to her."

Curtis winked at his mate. "Ah, his lady love!"

"Yes, she is, but she's a lot more than that," said Jak. "She's Titania's daughter, and if I don't get her back to the fairy queen, there's likely to be a war."

"Oh, dear!" said Doreen. "This sounds so complicated!"

"Speaking of complicated, do you think we should take the upper pass or Snake Valley?" Curtis asked Doreen.

"The upper pass is shorter," she replied.

"Then the upper pass it is!" said Curtis. "We'll just have to hope that Sinovia has gone to lunch."

"Who's Sinovia?"

"Another sphinx, but she's nothing like us," said Doreen. "She has wings."

The two sphinxes had been right when they told Jak that he would have gotten lost without their help. Soon after they started across the desert floor, the land dipped and they entered a series of twisting, turning chasms. They had walked for more than an hour when they came upon the end of a stone bridge that arced into the sky above the maze of canyons. The bridge was about four feet wide, so they walked single file up the middle with Curtis in the lead and Doreen bringing up the rear.

They had nearly reached the center of the bridge when Curtis exclaimed, "Drat, she's here. Ah, well, it was bound to happen sooner or later. Hello, Sinovia," he called in a louder voice. "How are you today?"

Peering around Curtis's back, Jak gulped and took a deep breath. This sphinx was indeed very different from Curtis and Doreen. It was true that she had eagle wings, but she also had the head and chest of a human woman, and apparently she didn't like wearing clothes. Jak tried to keep his gaze on her face.

"Hello, Curtis, Doreen," said Sinovia. "Who's that you have with you?"

"A friend of ours," said Curtis.

"Psst!" Doreen hissed from behind Jak. "Just keep moving. Whatever you do, don't let her trap you into trying to answer her riddles. She makes up impossible questions that only she can answer and then eats anyone who can't answer them. Hurry up; stay close to Curtis and you should be fine."

Jak nodded and darted forward until he was so close that Curtis's swishing tail slapped him on the legs. Curtis headed for the side of the bridge next to where Sinovia was standing, her feet firmly planted in the middle.

"Boy!" Sinovia said to Jak as he followed Curtis past her. "Tell me—how is a griffin like a turnip?"

"Keep going," muttered Doreen in Jak's ear.

Jak shuffled past Sinovia with his two friends so close that he was almost stepping on Curtis's heels and Doreen's feet were brushing against his.

"Here's an easy one," said Sinovia. "What hears everything, sees nothing, and is usually covered with hair?"

"Don't answer," Doreen told him in a fierce whisper.

A moment later they were past the winged sphinx and starting down the other side of the bridge.

"Wait! He's supposed to answer my riddle!" cried Sinovia.

"Not today," said Curtis. "We're in a hurry."

"But he's not supposed to pass by unless he gives the right answer. That's one of the rules!"

"They're your rules, Sinovia," called Doreen. "You made them up. Nobody has to follow them if they don't want to."

"But this is my bridge!" Sinovia shouted, stamping her foot.

"Only because you say it is," replied Doreen. "Have a nice afternoon. Give our regards to your mother."

"You can't do this!" the winged sphinx shrieked, launching herself at Jak.

Curtis and Doreen turned so they both stood in front of Jak. Growls rumbled in their throats, and when Sinovia got too close, Curtis swiped at her with claws extended. She backed off, her tail between her legs, and began to slink away.

Jak and his friends continued down the bridge, but they hadn't gone far when Sinovia called after them, "You won't get away with this! My mother will hear what you did. What's your name, boy?"

"Don't give her your real name," whispered Doreen. "You should never give your real name to creatures you can't trust."

"It's Nihlo!" Jak shouted. Nihlo was his nasty older cousin who had mistreated Jak since the day they met. The last time they'd seen each other, Nihlo had tried to kill him. If anyone deserved the wrath of a sphinx, it was Nihlo.

Jak and his two new friends stood together, watching as the winged sphinx spiraled in the air above them, calling them rude words, before flying off to the south.

"Who's her mother?" Jak asked a few minutes later as they reached the end of the bridge.

"A neighbor of my great-aunt Daphine," said Doreen. "Sinovia's mother is just like Sinovia, only she wouldn't have given in just then. She guards the Treeburnt Pass. Nobody goes there unless they absolutely have to."

Only a short distance past the bridge, the canyon opened out into a plain laced with freshwater springs and burbling streams. When Jak shaded his eyes with his hand, he could see a vast forest on the far side of the plain.

"Oberon's court lives in that forest," said Curtis.

"Then I'm almost there," said Jak. He started forward, but when the sphinxes didn't move to join him, he stopped and looked back. "Aren't you coming?"

Curtis shook his head. "This is as far as we go. We never enter the Land of Forgetfulness. That's part of it right there," he said, indicating the plain.

"If you go straight through, you'll be in it for only a few miles," said Doreen.

"I don't understand," said Jak. "I've seen a map of this area. It showed Sphinx Alley extending all the way to the forest."

"It used to," said Curtis, "but the Land of Forgetfulness has a way of shifting, almost as if it forgets where it's supposed to be."

"Is there any way around it?"

"Not unless you want to go through the Troll Woods, and we don't recommend that to anyone," said Doreen. "Now, before you go, there are a few things we think you should know. Be careful when you're around Oberon. The fairy king's magic is slyer than most. He likes to control people, and he does it by changing the way they see the world. If your lady love is there, he's probably used his magic on her. There is a way to undo it, however."

"That's right," Curtis said. "Just sprinkle pink fairy dust on her and say,

*Undo the spell*
*That someone used*
*To change her worldly view.*
*Allow her now*
*To clear her sight*
*And see that which is true.*

It's simple, but it works. She should regain all her memories and be her usual self."

"Where can I get this pink fairy dust?" asked Jak.

"You'll find it when you get there," said Curtis. "The pink dust has a lot of uses. It does whatever the user wants it to, from soothing a baby's bottom to making a spell work for someone who has no skill with magic."

Doreen gently cuffed Jak with her paw and kissed him on the cheek. "Good luck, dear boy. Thank you for helping my Curtis. We try to help others, but no one has ever come to our aid before. We're in your debt."

"Could you do me a favor then?" asked Jak. "Could you watch out for Tobi and help him if he comes this way?"

"Certainly!" said Doreen. "We'll do whatever we can."

"Farewell, young cat goblin," Curtis added, his voice sounding hoarser than usual. "May your friends be strong and your enemies lame."

"Thank you for everything," Jak told them both. "You've been a big help."

He was walking away, wondering how he could write a reminder, when he heard them talking behind him. "You talked to him more than I've ever heard you talk to a stranger before, Doreen," said Curtis.

"He's like the son we never had," Doreen said with a catch in her voice. "I don't want him to get hurt."

"We have fourteen cubs!" said Curtis. "Nine of them are boys. You said yourself that he reminds you of Tomi."

"Yes, but not even Tomi is quite like him."

"You mean a cat goblin?" Curtis asked.

"Precisely!" said Doreen.

Jak smiled. He would never forget all they had done to help him. Which reminded him . . . He reached into his pocket for the pencil and scrap of parchment that Tobi had found. The pencil was broken and the parchment was a sodden mess that fell apart in his hands, ruined when he'd crossed the river. Spoiled in the human world, Jak decided that a marker would work better than a broken pencil and took a moment to transmogrify it. The message would have to be short and not easily confused. On the back of one hand he wrote *HEAD FOR THE FOREST*. On the back of the other he wrote *GET TAMISIN*. Jak hesitated for a moment, trying to decide how to tell himself to hurry. Finally, he simply wrote *RUN!*

Satisfied that he could find Oberon's court once he reached any point in the forest, Jak put the marker away and took his first step into the Land of Forgetfulness.

# Chapter 13

Perched on one of the jumbled boulders just above the waves, Tamisin watched the setting sun turn the sky into such glorious shades of peach and pink and red that it didn't seem real. Although it was late and she knew she should be heading back, she wanted to be alone now to think. Irinia had warned her to be careful, and Dasras had told her that the fairies weren't to be trusted, but what she hadn't known was how much the fairies wanted to get rid of her.

Someone had to be behind all this, but who? One fairy? A group of fairies? She remembered reading a murder mystery where a whole trainload of people had tried to kill a single passenger. Was she getting unjustifiably paranoid, or were *all* the fairies against her? The only people who seemed to be willing to help her weren't fairies and had their own reasons for disliking fairy-kind.

Should she tell Oberon? If she decided to tell him, she should do it while they were alone, something that had yet to happen. Maybe she should tell Dasras. He spent a lot of time with Oberon and could relay the information to him. But what about Dasras himself? He had already told her that he was afraid that Oberon would tire of him someday and no longer treat him like a son. What if he was afraid that Tamisin might displace him in Oberon's affections? Malcolm the cobbler had told her that fairies were really just out for themselves, and she hadn't seen anything to disprove that. Dasras wasn't a fairy, but because fairies had raised him, there was no saying how much they had influenced him.

Tamisin was so confused that she didn't know what to think, and even began to doubt her own father. What if Oberon hadn't been completely truthful when he said he'd brought her here to get to know her? Maybe Oberon wanted her with him so Titania couldn't have her. Malcolm had said that he'd been brought to the court as much to keep other beings from getting his shoes as he was to make shoes for the fairies. Could Oberon be that heartless that he could think of her that way, too? The idea that Tamisin didn't know whom she could trust when she needed so desperately to trust someone had her stomach churning. Whatever the case, the best solution seemed to be to go home to the human world. Now if only she knew how to get there.

Loud voices made Tamisin glance down the beach. It was dusk, and in the half-light she could just make out a group of ogres stomping around the curve of the cove, headed in her direction. She narrowed her eyes, trying to see better. It was an ogress and two ogres, and all three were shouting at one another. The ogress was carrying a bundle in her arms while the two men shoved each other even as they walked.

"I wish neither of you had come here!" the woman cried. "I could have handled it myself!"

"Right!" said the older ogre. "As if you've done such a good job so far! I wouldn't have come if this lamebrain husband of yours hadn't made such a stink about fetching you home."

"I couldn't just leave her here, not after the baby was born!" the other ogre said. "Are you sure you won't come with me, Narlayna? They can always find someone else to make their stupid clothes!"

"She's here because she's my daughter!" the first ogre roared. "It will reflect badly on all of us if she leaves now. This whole thing is your fault, Bevin! No one gave you permission to have a conjugal visit last year!" With one mighty shove, the older ogre knocked the younger one off his feet and into an oncoming wave.

Bevin got to his feet spluttering. "Keep your grubby paws off me, Darlander!" he snarled. "She's my wife and you should never have made her come here!"

"You didn't marry her until after Oberon ordered her to court! You should have waited until her time of service was over."

"That won't be for years! We couldn't wait that long!"

"Stop it, both of you!" Narlayna said, patting the bundle in her arms. "This isn't about me or Bevin. It's about getting the baby home before the fairies know she's here! Do you know how many rules we broke when you came to visit me, Bevin? If they ever found out that I had a baby . . ." She glanced down at the little face peering up at her and her expression softened. "Where did you say you left your boats?" she asked the two male ogres.

Tamisin crouched down amid the rocks, making herself as small and inconspicuous as she could while the ogre family trudged past. They went only a short distance, however, before she heard their voices again. "If Narlayna's not going with us, we need only one boat," said Bevin. "Listen, Sweetness, I'll leave my boat here with you. Use it to come home if the fairies give you any trouble."

"Don't be a fool," Darlander growled. "You need that boat. If anyone is going to leave a boat for Narlayna, it should be me. I'll ride with you and hold the baby while you steer. And Narlayna, use the boat if you need to. We owe your labor to the king, but no one mistreats my little girl."

"Thank you, Father. I will."

Once Tamisin heard the sound of wood scraping on rock and saw the shadowy figures of the male ogres carrying a boat down to the water, she climbed up the rocks and down the other side, trying to be as quiet as possible. When she got close enough, she recognized the ogres as the two she had seen fighting earlier that day. She was still watching when the ogres climbed into the boat and Narlayna handed them the baby. Tamisin felt like crying, too, when she heard the ogress weeping. If all this was going on in Narlayna's life, it was no wonder the ogress had been upset the day Tamisin met her.

❦

Tamisin had reached the forest and was heading for the flat rock where supper was served, hoping Irinia hadn't cleared everything away yet, when she saw a cloud of tiny fairies advancing through the forest. Seeing that other full-sized fairies were hurrying out of their way, she moved to stand behind a tree.

"What's going on?" a fairy only a few yards away asked another. "Colonel Mountain Ash doesn't usually patrol our woods at night."

"Haven't you heard? Some ogres were spotted on our side of the hedge after curfew. I don't like ogres, but I'd hate to be one when the colonel catches them. He'll do his best to make an example of them so no one else tries anything."

Tamisin glanced back the way she had come. Narlayna's family was leaving, but the ogress was staying behind, which meant that if anyone was going to be caught, it would be her. From all that Tamisin had heard, Narlayna had enough problems without having to face the colonel, too.

Tamisin pretended to be as curious as the other fairies while the colonel and his troops were around, but as soon as she saw them fly off and knew that no one else was looking, she slipped back through the trees to the rocks by the cove. By the time she reached them, it was already dark. Once again she climbed over the rocks as quietly as she could, which was harder now that she couldn't really see where she was going. Keeping a low profile, she paused at the top to listen before climbing down the other side. At first all she could hear was the rumbling thunder of the waves breaking and the more muted sound of the water shushing across the sand. But after a few minutes she heard the soft, unmistakable sound of someone weeping. Peering into the darkness, she thought she saw a dark shape on the beach just past the waterline.

She had climbed partway down the rocks when she decided that it might not be wise to startle an ogress, so she began to make noise on purpose, pushing smaller rocks over, and muttering to herself as she looked for better footholds. The shape on the beach moved and got larger, as if the ogress had gotten to her feet.

"Wait!" Tamisin called softly as the figure began to walk away. Jumping off the rocks, she hurried to catch up.

"What are you doing here?" Narlayna growled.

"I want to help you," said Tamisin. "If you return to your cave now, Colonel Mountain Ash and his fairies will catch you. They want to make an example of you for being out after curfew."

"How do you know that?" asked the ogress, sounding more worried than angry.

Tamisin glanced back at the rocks. "Because I saw them, just like I saw you and your family earlier. Don't worry," she said, reaching for Narlayna's arm when the ogress began to edge away. "I'm not going to tell anyone. I just want to help you get back to your cave without anyone seeing you."

"I don't need your help," said Narlayna. "I know a path through the trees that will get me there just fine."

"If you're sure . . . ," said Tamisin. She watched as the ogress trudged away, going farther down the beach before turning inland. Tamisin frowned, annoyed with herself for being unable to make up her mind. The ogress might not want her help, but then, she didn't know exactly what she was facing. Narlayna was still upset and might do something that could get her hurt. At least Tamisin could stand as lookout for her. Silently, Tamisin followed Narlayna and was surprised when the ogress climbed an incline so steep that it was almost a vertical wall.

Tamisin ran to the wall and peered up. There were no hidden handholds or likely looking ledges where she could place her hands or feet. The wall was as sheer and smooth as something sanded by winter storms could be.

"I'm not climbing that!" Tamisin muttered to herself. "But then, I don't have to." With a shrug of her shoulders, she freed her wings and looked up. Moments later she was hovering in the air behind Narlayna, who had reached the top of the wall and was standing on a narrow ledge, peering into the forest. When the ogress didn't move, Tamisin looked past her to the twinkling lights drifting between the trees.

"I can still help you," she whispered to Narlayna.

The ogress turned her head sharply, then nodded and

started back down. When she reached the ground, she set her hands on her hips and looked Tamisin over. "Why do you want to help me? You don't know me. We aren't friends. I don't even like you."

"I can't help that," Tamisin said, shrugging. "I want to help you because I don't think the fairies are treating you right. People wouldn't put up with it back where I come from, and I don't like it here, either. Fairies may have more magic than anyone else, but that doesn't make them better."

Narlayna grunted and looked Tamisin in the eyes. "So what exactly do you think you can do for me?"

"The tree where I sleep isn't far from here. If we can get past the guards, I can hide you in my bed until morning. No one would think of looking for you there."

Narlayna snorted. "I'd never fit in one of those puny little beds! Even if I could, it would never support my weight. You're going to have to do better than that!"

"Then I don't know, unless . . . How do you feel about flying? The fairies are searching the forest, but they never seem to fly very high. If I fly higher, we might be able to get past without any of them spotting us. I doubt very much they would ever think of looking up. I could fly you to your cave and they would never know that you hadn't been there all along."

"You're going to turn into one of those itty-bitty little things and lift me?" said Narlayna. "I don't think so!"

"Am I itty-bitty now?" asked Tamisin. "Because I'm not going to get any smaller than this."

"Fairies can't fly very far when they're your size. I'm

162

surprised you flew all the way up there," Narlayna said, glancing at the rock wall. "There's no way a big fairy could fly all the way to the hedge lugging a dandelion, let alone me!"

"If you haven't noticed yet, I'm not a normal fairy," said Tamisin. "I'm bigger than most and so are my wings. I've carried a person before without any trouble."

"I bet that person wasn't an ogress."

"Well, no, but that doesn't mean I can't. It's at least worth a try."

"And if you can't?"

"Then we'll think of something else. Why are you complaining? All you have to do is hold on. I'm the one who's going to do all the work." Stepping closer to the ogress, Tamisin raised her arms and said, "Wrap your arms around my waist and we'll see if I can do this."

Narlayna laughed even as she reached for Tamisin. "You'll never be able to get off the ground, let alone carry me above the trees!"

She was still chuckling when Tamisin said, "Hold on tight and don't look down."

"What are you talking about? I . . . How did you do that?" said the ogress, glancing down past her feet to the tops of the trees below. Suddenly she was squeezing Tamisin so hard that the girl could scarcely breathe.

"Not so . . . tight!" Tamisin gasped.

"Sorry," Narlayna said, loosening her grip. "Wow!" she added, looking around. "I've never been this high. You're a lot stronger than you look."

"Can't talk now!" wheezed Tamisin, who was already regretting her offer to carry the ogress. Not only was Narlayna big but ogres were solid and weighed even more than a human the same size would have weighed.

Tamisin's heart was racing, and her breath was coming in ragged gasps as she glanced down to make sure she was going the right way. In the light of the nearly full moon she could make out the silver ribbon of the stream and the thick dark line of the hedge just beyond it. The fairies' side of the forest was filled with twinkling lights, whereas the other side was much darker.

*Just a little farther,* Tamisin thought, although the hedge looked miles away.

"This is incredible!" said Narlayna. "Why didn't I do this before?"

Tamisin chuckled, which turned into a gasp of pain. She was straining something in her back, and the pain was only getting worse. Suddenly it felt as if something tore; the pain was so intense that she could barely see straight. "We have to . . . set down," she said, but she was losing control as one of her wings refused to move the way she wanted it to. Using all her strength, Tamisin beat her wings as hard as she could, carrying them over the briar hedge even as they started to go down. She could see the glint of water, and thought they might be near the pool where she had seen the nymphs washing clothes. Then the ground hit and only Narlayna's strong arms kept Tamisin from tumbling over and over, a move that would have crushed her outstretched wings.

When Narlayna let go of her, Tamisin fell to her knees, her body shaking with pain. The ogress took one look at her and picked her up like she would a small child. The pain was so intense that Tamisin couldn't think of anything else. Squeezing her eyes shut, she gritted her teeth as the ogress ran with a lumbering gait. Tamisin didn't open her eyes again until they entered Narlayna's cave and the ogress laid her on a bed so soft that the down mattress seemed to swallow her.

Tamisin sat up once when the ogress made her swallow something sweet and thick. Her entire body became numb a few minutes later, and she drifted off to sleep even as Narlayna spoke to someone in a half whisper. When she woke again, it was still dark, but a candle lit the cave enough that Tamisin could see Irinia bending over her. The two-faced woman gave her another drink, but this one was bitter and made Tamisin's tongue feel like it was too big for her mouth. Irinia was spreading something cold and sticky on Tamisin's back when she fell asleep again. A short time later she dreamed of demanding voices and Narlayna speaking in a quiet, reasonable tone while Irinia sat beside her, holding her hand and warning her to be quiet.

*Why wouldn't I be?* Tamisin thought, and drifted into an even deeper sleep.

# Chapter 14

Jak was thinking about Tamisin when he started across the plain. Doreen's information about the fairy king had disturbed Jak more than he would have admitted. Although he had been worried about Tamisin before, he was worried in a different way now. What *did* Oberon want with her? And what did Doreen mean when she said that the fairy king changed how people looked at the world? It was true that Jak wasn't happy about the way Tamisin had turned away from him, but that had been her choice and she'd been free to make it. Jak hated the idea that Oberon might have changed her in any way. He was sure that Tamisin would have fought it, if she'd known what was going on. He'd have to start looking for the pink dust right away.

Jak glanced back and noticed that he'd already walked a good distance. He could no longer see the opening to the canyon where he'd left the two sphinxes. The land he was crossing now was covered with lush grass, more like a lawn in the human world than the tall grass in the Sograssy Sea.

Jak looked up; the forest didn't seem that far away now. He wondered when he'd start forgetting things. Maybe he wouldn't if he kept the important things fresh in his mind. His name was Jak, he was half human, half cat goblin, he was in love with a beautiful half fairy named Tamisin, and he was going to the forest to get her. For a moment he was worried when he couldn't remember why she was in the forest, but then he decided that it really didn't matter, as long as he knew that he had to go there because . . .

Jak scraped his fingers through his hair and frowned. There was something on the edge of his mind that he knew was important, but he couldn't remember what. Oh well, he remembered that he was going to get his girl-friend, who . . . It bothered Jak that he could no longer remember her name, but that wasn't the important part. As long as he remembered that he had to go to . . .

Jak stopped in midstep and looked around. He knew he had come here to do something, but he couldn't remember what. Tired and thirsty, he decided to sit down for a minute. He chose a spot beside a narrow stream where the water looked fresh and inviting. Bending down beside the water, he set his hand on something hidden in the grass. It was smoother than a rock, and rounded. Curious, he brushed the grass aside. It wasn't a rock at all, but a skull. Jak scrambled to his feet, his thirst forgotten.

Movement caught his eye, and he turned his head in

time to see a large creature with the head of a man and a catlike body the size of a pony slinking belly-to-ground, its golden eyes fastened on him. He thought it might be a sphinx until he saw the fur-covered ball of bone on the end of its tail. Jak knew that manticores were common in certain parts of the land of the fey, but he'd always avoided such places. Because he'd never had firsthand experience with the beasts before, he wasn't sure what to do, so he did the only thing he could think of: he ran.

The moment Jak started running, the manticore rose from its crouch and took off after him. Jak could hear it bounding across the ground behind him, its paws making a muffled *thud-thud, thud-thud* in the grass. He glanced back to see how close it was and with the next step tumbled into a creek whose flowing water had eroded the ground a few feet below the land around it. Startled, a pair of ducks erupted from the water and flew away with a whir of wings.

Lying sprawled on his stomach in the shallow water, Jak squeezed his eyes shut and waited for the manticore to pounce. After a time, when nothing happened, he drank from the stream, quenching the thirst he'd momentarily forgotten. When he sat up, he noticed a lionlike beast chasing two ducks deeper into the Land of Forgetfulness.

Setting his hands on the raised ground in front of him, Jak started to stand when he noticed the writing. *HEAD FOR THE FOREST*, read the back of one hand. *GET TAMISIN*, read the other. Beneath it was written, *RUN!*

*Oh, right*, thought Jak. He looked around. There was a

forest in that direction. Although he couldn't remember why he needed to go there, he knew it must be important if he'd written it down. As for Tamisin, he had no idea who or what Tamisin might be, but if he came across one, he'd be sure to get it.

Jak began to run, but soon slowed his pace to a walk. He hadn't gone far when the sound of laughter made him turn his head. Only a dozen yards away a little raccoon goblin was doing cartwheels across the grass, chortling to himself. Turning one time too many, he landed in a stream with a splash, but instead of getting upset, the goblin only laughed louder.

Curious, Jak started toward the goblin. When he reached the side of the stream, he found the goblin crouched in the water, trying to scoop up the tiny silver fish that darted around his ankles. Suddenly the goblin's hands shot forward and came up with a dozen squirming silver bodies. Popping them all into his mouth at once, he sat down in the stream, chewing, with a contented expression on his face.

Jak's stomach was rumbling, so he waded into the stream to catch his own fish. There were so many in the water that Jak was soon nibbling some, too.

"What are you doing?" asked the raccoon goblin.

Jak swallowed his last bite. "Eating," he replied. For a moment he thought the little goblin looked familiar, but the thought melted away when he spotted more fish.

A fish nipped the raccoon goblin's leg. When the goblin glanced down, his eyes lit up. "Look! Fish!" He rolled over onto his knees and lunged, catching some in each hand.

Jak was bending down to try for another fish when a meandering butterfly flew past. Following the butterfly with his eyes, he spotted a patch of wildflowers. A moment later he had splashed his way out of the water and was on his knees, picking wildflowers to give to . . . someone. Once again he noticed the writing on his hands. Once again he stood and ran toward the forest.

It was dusk when Jak approached the edge of the Land of Forgetfulness. The trees of the forest looked especially forbidding as the sun set behind them, and he felt a sudden reluctance to leave the grassland. Instead, he found a dry spot where moss made a comfortable bed beside a gurgling stream, and sat down, turning his back to the forest. He didn't notice the tiny lights that twinkled at regular intervals under the last of the trees, nor did he see that more gathered there as the night grew darker.

Jak couldn't remember when he'd eaten last, but then, he couldn't remember much of anything. His stomach was a little upset, so he lay back, pillowing his head on his arms. Something was wrong, he just didn't know what, but he was sure that he'd figure it all out tomorrow.

# Chapter 15

Tamisin sat up and groaned, then realized that though she felt stiff all over and had an awful taste in her mouth, the terrible pain in her back was gone, leaving an ache no worse than when she'd pulled a muscle back home. Even before she opened her eyes, she remembered where she was and how she'd gotten there, although she was a bit fuzzy about what had happened after she and Narlayna reached the cave.

When she looked around, the light and airy space confused her because it wasn't at all cavelike. The room itself wasn't very big, but it was filled with sunlight angled in with mirrors near the opening at the front of the cave. Other mirrors fastened to the walls reflected the light, bouncing it back and forth so that it was nearly as bright inside as out. Fresh flowers filled bowls, vases, and jars on every available surface. Baskets overflowing with flower petals lined the back wall. With so many flowers, the cave smelled like a garden in springtime, and Tamisin half expected to see butterflies searching for nectar. The one thing that Tamisin didn't see was another person.

"Narlayna?" she called as she climbed off the down mattress that filled one corner of the room. When there was no reply, she tiptoed to a curtain hung on the back wall, thinking the ogress might be sleeping inside, but the storage space was empty save for a few boxes and trunks.

So much had happened the day before that it seemed as if everything should have changed, but she doubted that anything would be different on the other side of the briar hedge. At least she knew what she had to do now; she'd ask Oberon to have someone escort her back to the human world.

Tamisin still wanted to thank Narlayna for taking care of her, so she looked for her outside the cave entrance. When the ogress wasn't there either, Tamisin took the path back to the opening in the briar hedge. She was passing through the deep shadows of tall pine trees when she smelled a pungent odor that cut through the fresh scent of pine and made her eyes water. She recognized the stench of troll, having smelled it the last time she was in the land of the fey, so she stopped and began to back away. Before she'd taken more than a few steps, a troll lurched out from behind a tree and grabbed her arm with one of his meaty hands.

"I . . . ," he cried.

". . . got her!" shouted a different voice as a second hand clamped down on her other arm.

Tamisin twisted around and saw that the two-headed troll was nasty looking and, though shorter than she was, much broader across the shoulders and back. It was obvious he hadn't bathed in a long time, if ever, and his long, greasy hair was crawling with bugs. One head had an equally filthy beard dangling past his knees, and the other had crusty nose hairs so long that they covered his upper lip, mouth, and chin.

"Let go of me!" Tamisin screamed, and kicked out behind her with all her strength. Her foot connected and she yelped. It felt as if she'd kicked a solid tree trunk.

One of the heads grunted as the troll dragged her off the path and deeper into the pine trees. Tamisin struggled, throwing herself against his tightening grip until it felt as though his fingers were digging into her bone. Knowing that she wasn't defenseless, Tamisin was more disgusted than afraid; she could imagine the bugs crawling off the troll and into her hair.

She let herself get angry, and was pleased when the sky darkened. The troll hustled her down a short slope past a mound of trailing vines that had been ripped up, roots and all, to the shadowed entrance of a cave. Thunder boomed as he shoved her through the narrow opening and flung her on the floor where she lay, sprawled, for a fraction of a second before scrambling to her feet.

It hadn't occurred to Tamisin that he might be able to get her inside so quickly, and without enough weather to help her, she no longer felt quite so brave. *Get a weapon*, she thought, studying the floor of the darkened cave as best she could while trying to keep her distance from the troll. Other than a filthy blanket, the ashes of a cold fire, and some broken and gnawed animal bones, there was little in the cave to show that anyone lived there.

Tamisin thought about trying to run past the troll, but that thought died quickly when she saw how his chunky body blocked the opening. Thunder boomed and lightning flashed outside, but the troll didn't seem to care. If only she could zap him with a bolt of lightning!

"Let's roast . . . ," one troll head began.

". . . the girl," said the other.

". . . for dinner!" the first head finished.

"Yummy!" they both declared, patting their ponderous belly in unison.

"We start fire . . ."

". . . wrap her in leaves . . ."

". . . tuck her in coals . . ."

". . . and bake her!"

Unable to see anything in the depths of the cave, Tamisin slowly felt her way backward with her foot, inching away from the lip-smacking troll. She watched as he banged two rocks together, trying to light a small piece of tinder. When he finally had a spark, the heads took turns blowing gently on the tiny flame.

Suddenly, Tamisin had an idea. It wouldn't be easy to guide the barest whisper of wind into the cave. She'd have to aim it just so through the entrance and draw it all the way back to the fire, but all she needed was one small puff . . .

The troll sat back, a dumbfounded look on both of his faces. "You blew . . ."

". . . fire out!" the two heads accused each other.

"Did not!" said one.

"Me neither!" said the other.

"We try . . ."

". . . again!"

While the troll went through the steps of lighting a fire all over again, Tamisin got down on her hands and knees, feeling the ground for a loose rock or anything she could use as a weapon. When her hand finally closed on a stick, she almost dropped it when she picked it up and realized that it was actually a leg bone with a knob at one end. *But,* she thought, *it would work,* and she stood, holding the bone behind her back. Once more she waited until the troll had the fire started; she blew it out with a gentle puff of air.

As thunder boomed so loudly that the cave itself shook, the troll got to his feet and his two heads turned to each other.

"Why you . . ."

". . . keep doing that?"

"It not me!"

"It you!"

Both heads were frowning as they glanced down at the cold ashes. "I know!" said one, his expression brightening. "We eat girl raw!"

"I going to say that!" said the other.

"Good idea!" said the first.

The second troll beamed. "I know!"

Tamisin shrank back when the troll turned in her

175

direction. He was only a few feet away when she drew the bone from behind her back, raised it high, and brought it down on the bearded troll's head with a loud *crack!* Although it was the bone that broke and not the troll's skull, the bearded troll howled at the top of his lungs. Tamisin zigzagged as he came after her, his arms grabbing, both heads wailing. Although she was able to duck under his outstretched arms, the troll stayed between her and the opening of the cave.

There was a flurry of movement by the door, and Malcolm the brownie tore into the cave, stumbled, and fell flat on the floor. Tamisin saw him, but the troll didn't, and with an angry shout and a flailing of arms, the troll tripped over the brownie and landed faces-down on the rough stone floor. Before the troll could get to his feet, Narlayna was there, too, plunking herself down on the troll's back. The troll continued to holler, flopping his arms and kicking his legs, but the ogress just smiled and patted his two heads as she made herself more comfortable.

"Quiet down, pea brain!" she told the troll. When she glanced up and saw Tamisin standing there, staring open-mouthed with surprise, Narlayna shook her head in exasperation and yelled, "Run! I'm not going to sit here all day!"

"That not fair!" shouted the troll. "Fairy say I can eat girl!"

"Really?" Narlayna said as Tamisin headed for the cave entrance. "And which fairy was that?"

"Come on!" Malcolm hollered as he tugged on Tamisin's hand. She turned and ran with him, out the narrow cave opening, around the pile of leafy debris, onto the path, and back to Narlayna's home. "We'll wait here for Narlayna," the brownie told her. "She wanted to talk to you before you went back to the other side of the hedge."

"There's no door," Tamisin said as they stepped inside the cozy cave.

"There's no door been built that can keep a troll out, but he'd know from the smell of it that this place belongs to an ogre, so he wouldn't follow us in here even at night," said the brownie. "Ogres are the only thing trolls fear, aside from sea monsters and sunlight. Sea monsters because they can hold their breath longer than trolls and can hold them down and drown them, and sunlight because it turns trolls into stone. Did you notice how dark that troll's cave was and that he stayed in the shadows of the pine forest?"

"Why are trolls afraid of ogres?" asked Tamisin.

"Because ogres aren't afraid of them," said Malcolm. "Ogres are bigger and stronger. They're smarter, too, but then, just about everybody is smarter than a troll. Even so, only ogres can take on a full-sized troll. If I knew a troll was after me, I'd skedaddle out of this forest so fast that a jackrabbit couldn't keep up with me."

"That's his way of saying that he thinks you should leave Oberon's court as soon as you can," Narlayna said as she stepped into her cave. "Whoever sent that troll after you isn't trying to be subtle."

Malcolm nodded. "We didn't know there was a new troll in the woods until we heard him howl. If we hadn't come running, you would have been his next meal. The only troll that's supposed to be here is old Ingebert, who takes care of the bridges, and he's bad enough. Now we're going to have to go to all the effort of driving this new one out or he'll make no end of trouble."

"The troll said a fairy told him he could eat me," Tamisin said, shuddering at the thought. "Did he tell you which fairy?"

Narlayna shook her head. "The troll didn't say much of anything, except that a male fairy lured him here by offering you up as dinner. Apparently the troll can tell males and females apart, but other than that he thinks all fairies look alike, except for you. He said you look more human than the rest, so you were easy to recognize. I was able to stop him for now, but he still plans to hunt you down."

"The fairy who sent the troll after you isn't the only one who means you harm," said Malcolm. "Fairies talk when they think they're alone, and I have a way of blending into the trees. I know of at least two fairies who were involved in the incident with the sea monster and three others who moved the porpoise, not including the one who talked to the mermaid. Then there were the nasty pieces of work who tried to get you to eat the frillet berries. If you stick around, one of them is bound to succeed sooner or later."

"I already plan on leaving. I'm going to ask my father to have Mountain Ash take me home."

"When you mention your father, do you mean Oberon?" said the brownie.

Tamisin frowned. "Yes, of course. Why do you ask?"

Malcolm and Narlayna exchanged glances. It was the ogress who spoke up. "Because some of us have doubts that he really is your father. There's no denying that Titania is your mother, but you're too much like a human—"

"And better for it," interrupted Malcolm.

"To be a full-blood fairy," Narlayna concluded.

"I know he's my father! Oberon—"

"Has his own way of shaping the truth," said Narlayna. "He probably used his magic to convince you."

Tamisin sighed. "Why not? I'm sure Dasras used magic to make me think I loved him. I suppose if Oberon gives me a hard time, I could fly back to Titania's forest on my own. The gates near her forest open up close to where I live in the human world. I'd just need someone to show me the way."

"You'd never make it," said Malcolm. "The only ones who can fly away from Oberon's forest are the fairies who shrink themselves down till they're so small that most of the bigger monsters can't even see them. We've heard that you can't change your size, so you'd be the first thing the beasties would go after. That's why Mountain Ash had to shrink you before flying all the way back here."

Narlayna nodded. "Every direction has its risks. The Southern Sea is to the south. No one goes in that direction if they can help it. There are too many nasty creatures in the sea, and some of the larger monsters are able to leap out of the water to surprising heights. You can't fly west along the shore without running into the Land of Forgetfulness. If you try crossing over it, by land or by air, you'll lose your memory. If you stay there long enough, you'll lose your life as well."

"And to the east?"

"Griffins. Most griffins live north on the Griffin Hunting Grounds except for a few colonies, one of which lives here. Go beyond the griffins and you'll reach dragon territory. And in that direction is Sphinx Alley," she said, pointing directly north. "Don't go that way either. The sphinxes like to waylay everyone and ask crazy riddles. If you don't give them the answer they want, they'll eat you. If they don't like the way you give the answer, they'll eat you. Of course, they're not all like that, just the ones you're likely to meet."

"So in other words, there's no way to leave Oberon's forest," said Tamisin.

"Not without help," the ogress said.

"You could leave tonight during the dance. That will give us time to find someone to take you home, and the dance itself will be enough of a distraction for you to slip away," Malcolm told her. "In the meantime, be discreet. There's no saying what the fairies who don't like you might do if they knew you were leaving. Some might be satisfied that you're going, but others might want to make sure you can never come back. There's something else," he said, glancing at Narlayna. When the ogress nodded, the brownie continued. "We've heard rumors that Titania found out that Oberon had you kidnapped and is as mad as a hornet on a hot frying pan. Word is out that she's on her way here."

"Then I can go back with her!" said Tamisin.

"Maybe, maybe not," said Malcolm. "Her showing up might just be the worst thing that could happen. The last time they fought, they destroyed a lovely forest just north of here. They ravaged the ground so thoroughly that nothing will ever grow there again. What used to be called Ever Green Forest is now Griffin Alley. Believe me, no one is safe when fairy royalty fight."

# Chapter 16

Jak woke the next morning to the sun shining in his eyes and the feeling that he had something important to do, only he had no idea what it might be. Yawning, he sat up, stretched, and looked around. It was a beautiful, calm day with a cloudless sky; Jak would have relished the thought of exploring the plain if he hadn't felt so uneasy.

He was getting to his feet when he noticed the writing on his hands. Turning in place, he saw that the forest began only a short distance away. The day was already getting hot and the shade looked tempting. He entered the forest a few minutes later and noticed how much cooler it was in the deep shade. He paused to look up, awed at the sight of the oldest trees he'd ever seen. Even the trunk of the smallest tree was so wide that three men could not circle it with their arms; most of the trees were far more massive.

This forest felt different than most. The air was heavy

with the breath of trees, the weight of their years, and something even harder to discern, which he finally decided was the tingle of magic. *It must be strong here if I can feel it*, he thought.

A flicker of movement drew Jak's eyes, and he saw a full-sized fairy warrior standing only a few feet away, watching him. The pinecones embroidered on the shoulder of his tunic indicated that the fairy was an officer. Two tiny fairies flitted around Jak, as if waiting to be told what to do. At the officer's gesture, the air sparkled and two warriors stood on either side of Jak, aiming short, slender reeds at him. Although the new arrivals didn't have the pinecone insignia, all three fairies were dressed in the colors of the trees around them; the browns and greens shifted as they moved, matching the trees and making the fairies hard to see.

"Hey, how are you doing?" said Jak, still used to the ways of humans. His memory was returning bit by bit, just enough to know that there was a lot he couldn't remember.

"What are you doing here, goblin?" asked the officer.

Jak wasn't sure what to say. He knew he had come to the forest for a reason, but he didn't have a clue what it might be.

"I'm not sure why I'm here," he replied.

The officer grunted. "It's too soon. He probably doesn't have his memory back yet. The effects of the Land of Forgetfulness don't wear off right away."

"How long will it take?" asked one of the other fairies.

"It varies, depending on the species, age, size . . . There's really no way to predict," the officer said, looking Jak up and down. "Can you tell us your name?" he asked Jak.

Jak could see from the suspicion in their eyes that the fairies didn't trust him, which made him think that he shouldn't trust them either. Something that he had heard recently crept into his mind, and he considered it good advice: don't give your real name to anyone you don't trust. He still couldn't remember his real name, but there was a name that he *knew* wasn't his. "Nihlo."

A twinkling light appeared in the gloom of the forest, darting under branches and over fallen trunks. It came to a stop beside the officer, and hovered there. The officer nodded and extended his hand. A moment later he was holding a pale yellow blossom and the tiny fairy was leaving.

"Say 'Ah,'" the officer said to Jak.

"Huh?" Jak replied.

The fairy squeezed the base of the blossom, squirting nectar into Jak's mouth. "That's good enough."

Jak opened his mouth to ask what was going on, but nothing would come out.

"I think it's working," said the officer. "We can ask him questions now, and he'll have to answer with the truth, whether or not he can consciously remember it himself. All right, goblin . . . You are a goblin, aren't you?"

Jak wanted to protest and say that they had no right to treat him this way, but he didn't seem to have any control over his voice. His mouth opened of its own accord and words came out, even though he wasn't thinking them. "I'm half cat goblin, half human."

"I thought he was a cat goblin, Lieutenant Spruce," said one of the other fairies. "They all have a certain look about them. I can honestly say that I can't tell them apart."

The other fairy snorted. "Look at him, Ragweed! He's half human! That's even worse than a full goblin. What's Titania going to send next—full humans?"

"That's enough of that, Mugwort," said the lieutenant before turning back to Jak. "Are you a spy?"

There were a lot of things that Jak wanted to say, but the only word that would come out was "No."

"Did Titania send you here?" asked the lieutenant.

"No."

"Then who did?"

"No one."

Mugwort made a rude sound. "This is worse than coaxing buds to open before their time!"

"Shh!" said Ragweed while the lieutenant scowled at Mugwort.

Turning back to Jak, Lieutenant Spruce asked, "Why did you come?"

"To see Princess Tamisin."

"Now we're getting somewhere!" breathed Mugwort. Ragweed punched his friend in the arm.

"Why did you come to see Princess Tamisin?" asked the lieutenant.

"Because I love her."

Mugwort snorted. "Yeah, right!"

"Don't laugh!" said Ragweed. "It has to be the truth if he said it under the influence of nectar."

"Do you intend to harm the princess?" Spruce asked Jak.

"No."

"Do you intend to harm anyone else here?"

"No."

"You can take him to the colonel now," Spruce told the two fairies. "Mountain Ash can decide what he wants to do with him."

Mugwort looked disappointed and shoved Jak when he didn't move quickly enough. "Leave him alone," said Ragweed. "We're just escorting him. He's not a prisoner."

"Yet," Mugwort muttered.

When Jak looked confused, Ragweed patted him on the back. "Don't listen to him. You're fine. Now all you have to do is talk to the colonel and he might let you see the princess. I'll take him myself," he told his friend as he led Jak away.

# Chapter 17

Tamisin would have preferred to fly over the briars, but her wing still hurt, and Narlayna told her not to use it for a few days. Instead the ogress escorted her as far as the opening in the hedge, where she stayed while Tamisin continued on. Upon reaching the clearing, Tamisin was surprised to see that the sun was high in the sky; she had missed breakfast as well as supper, so she headed toward the rock to try to get something to eat.

When she arrived, only a few fairies were helping themselves to food, but Irinia was there, and Tamisin remembered the two-faced woman's soothing touch the night before. Tamisin waited until Irinia noticed her before going closer and saying, "I want to thank you."

Irinia held up her hand in a shushing motion. "There's no need."

"Have you decided what you're going to wear to the dance?" one of the fairies asked another.

"My pink petal dress, of course," the fairy replied as they wandered off together.

Tamisin was about to try talking to Irinia again when Dasras hailed her.

"Where have you been?" he asked, scowling. "I went to your tree first thing this morning, but you weren't there. I've been looking all over for you."

"I got up early this morning and went for a walk," said Tamisin.

"I saw Buttercup by the lake. She said she saw you returning from the other side of the briar hedge."

Tamisin tried to think of an answer that wouldn't give too much away. "I went to ask Narlayna to make me a dress for the dance," she said, glancing at Irinia as she said it.

Irinia nodded and gave Tamisin a quick half smile.

"Ah," Dasras said, appearing satisfied. "Then you're going with me?"

"I guess I am." Tamisin groaned under her breath. She'd talked herself into a corner; now she'd either have to go or leave the forest before the dance began.

Plucking a fat, red apple from the table, she tried to think of something to say to Dasras. She no longer felt as if she loved him; the little voice telling her that she did had died on the mermaid's beach. There were a lot of things that she wanted to say to him, but none of them were pleasant, and she remembered Malcolm's warning to be discreet. Telling him off would attract attention, as would starting an argument, so neither one would be a good idea now. Instead, she took a bite from the apple, delaying the need to say anything, and looked up when a tiny messenger fairy arrived.

Instead of going to Dasras, the fairy came to her. She waited while he grew to full size. "Colonel Mountain Ash wants to see you," said the messenger. "Go to the fairy king's clearing. The colonel is waiting for you there."

"Why would the colonel want to see me?" she asked Dasras as the messenger flew away.

He shrugged. "I have no idea, but you should hurry. If the colonel wants to see you, it must be important."

# Chapter 18

Jak expected to go directly to the colonel, but instead Ragweed led the way to the middle of a briar patch and told him to wait there. After Ragweed left, Jak tried to say a few words out loud, but it took some time before he could use his own voice. His memory was coming back, too. He remembered who he was, that he had given the fairies a false name, and that he had come to get Tamisin. When he remembered how she had rejected him, he almost wished his memory hadn't come back so completely.

After a while Jak stood to stretch his legs and peeked out of the entrance to the briar patch. Ragweed was standing at the far end, peering back the way they had come. He stopped a passing fairy who gestured wildly, obviously agitated. Ragweed began to pace after the other fairy left, but it wasn't until a tiny fairy flew up to Ragweed and hovered by his ear that the big fairy finally became small and zipped away, leaving Jak in the briar patch unguarded.

❦

Tamisin walked so fast that she was nearly running. Something had happened, she was sure of it. Could Titania have come for her? Could something have happened to Oberon? Maybe bad news had made its way from the human world and something had happened to her adoptive family. The thought that something bad might have befallen one of the people she loved made Tamisin's breath catch in her throat.

The fog that had obscured the glade after Tamisin's last visit was gone when she arrived, and she could see Mountain Ash waiting for her. "It seems you have a visitor," the colonel said when she stood before him. "A cat-goblin boy has come to see you."

Tamisin could see that Mountain Ash was watching to see her reaction. She took a deep breath, willing her heartbeat to slow and her cheeks to cool. "Who is it?" she asked.

"He says his name is Nihlo. Do you know someone by that name?"

Tamisin was disappointed and more than a little afraid. When she'd heard it was a cat goblin, she'd begun to hope for a moment that it was someone else, someone whose name she couldn't remember. *Could the boy I can't remember be a cat goblin?* she wondered, surprised at her own reaction.

She remembered Nihlo, though, and her lip curled in dislike. "I know him."

Nihlo had wanted to kill her the last time she'd seen him. After leaving the land of the fey, she'd hoped that she'd never see him again. And now he was here. Tamisin was tempted to say that she didn't want to see him, but with so many guards around she didn't think he could hurt her. Besides, she was more than a little curious about why he would come so far.

A messenger fairy darted through the trees to hover beside the colonel. Mountain Ash held up one finger, motioning for the messenger to wait. "Tell me, what is Nihlo's relationship to Titania?" he asked Tamisin. "Does he work for her?"

Tamisin shook her head. "No. As far as I know, Nihlo doesn't work for anyone but Nihlo. He hates Titania and would hurt her if he could."

Another messenger arrived, and another and another. They hovered in the air beside Mountain Ash, their twinkling lights quivering with the urgency of their messages.

"Just a moment," Mountain Ash told Tamisin, and glanced at the fairy who had arrived first. His expression grew grimmer as he listened to the messenger. When the fairy finished, Mountain Ash turned to Tamisin. "You'll have to excuse me. Titania's forces have reached our border and have already mounted an attack. We'll talk more about your friend later." In an instant, Mountain Ash was as small as the messenger fairies and flying off with them.

Tamisin didn't know what to do. Her mother's army

was attacking her father's court? She'd heard of family squabbles, but nothing like this! Dasras had said that Titania loved her kingdom more than Tamisin or himself. However, if the fairy queen was deliberately starting a fight over her, Titania must love her more than the kingdom, or Oberon, or the fairies who were sure to get hurt in such a battle. Irinia and Narlayna had told Tamisin how fiercely Titania and Oberon could fight; the last thing Tamisin wanted was for anyone to get hurt because of her.

As much as she wanted to go home to the human world, she had to do something to keep Titania and Oberon from fighting. Would it help if she went to talk to them? But how would she get to her mother, and who knew where her father was now? Would they even listen to her if she could find them?

※

Jak was about to go in search of Tamisin when a small figure dressed all in brown appeared. "Come with me," the brownie said, gesturing for him to follow.

"Why?" said Jak.

The little man set his hands on his hips and rolled his eyes. "Because I'm trying to help you, you big galumphing idiot! I heard the fairies. You were supposed to talk to Mountain Ash before he'd let you see the princess, but something came up and he had to go. The fairies were going to leave you here, twiddling your thumbs. Fine, if you don't want my help, you can sit here and wait for your guard to come back. It's too bad, though. The princess Tamisin needs someone to help her, and I thought you might be the one."

"I'm coming!" said Jak as he hurried to catch up with the brownie, who could move surprisingly fast for someone with such short legs. "Are you a friend of Tamisin's?"

The brownie looked surprised at the question. After a moment's thought, he flashed a quick smile at Jak and said, "Yes, I guess you could say that I am."

They paused at the forest trail. When they didn't see anyone, they crept along the path, moving silently. Jak's heart leaped in his chest when he saw a solitary figure and realized that it was Tamisin. The brownie slipped away as Jak started running. "Tamisin!" he shouted. "I'm here!"

At the sound of the familiar voice, Tamisin's heart lurched and she felt a rush of excitement as she turned around, only to see a face she didn't recognize. The emotions that filled her as he approached were staggering, but she was so confused that she couldn't speak at first. Part of her wanted to run to him and throw herself into his arms, but another part told her to be cautious, that this was a stranger she'd never seen before. True, he was a cat goblin, but not the one she was expecting.

"You're not Nihlo," she said, taking a step back. She hated Nihlo; although she felt conflicting emotions when she saw this boy, hatred wasn't one of them.

# Chapter 19

Jak stopped in his tracks, stunned. "What? Tam, it's me! I came looking for you. Is something wrong?" he added when she retreated from him again.

"I'm sorry," she said, shaking her head. "I don't think we've ever met."

Jak was horrified. Either the fairies had sent her to the Land of Forgetfulness and her memories hadn't come back, or Oberon had used his magic on her and made her forget people. It couldn't be all her memories, though; if she knew he wasn't Nihlo, she must remember his cousin, at least. Jak decided that Oberon must be to blame if her memory loss was so selective.

"We met at Worthington Academy; don't you remember?" he said. "We ran into each other in the hallway—literally!"

"I know the academy, but I never met you there," Tamisin said, rubbing her forehead as if it hurt. "Listen, I don't know why you're here, but this isn't a good time.

There's a lot going on now and I have to talk to my father."

Although Jak's first instinct was to pull her into his arms, cover her face with kisses, and tell her that everything was going to be all right, he was afraid it would frighten her if she truly didn't remember him. Instead he watched her walk away, hoping that she would stop to look back at him, and he felt a tightness in his chest when she didn't. It was bad enough when she didn't want to be with him, but even worse to see her not know him at all.

And what did Tamisin mean when she said that she was going to talk to her father? Tamisin had told Jak that her real father was human and had died years before. Could she have learned something new? Did she think that Oberon was her father? Maybe she was talking about someone else.

Jak began to follow Tamisin. He didn't want her to see him trailing her, but he wasn't about to let her get out of sight, so he waited until she'd turned a corner in the path before hurrying after her. Slipping into the trees, he followed far enough off the path that she wouldn't see him if she did look back.

Although he knew he needed to look for the pink fairy dust and do what the sphinxes had suggested, he was reluctant to lose track of Tamisin until he knew more. It became harder to hide as they reached a more populated part of the forest. After almost tripping over a brownie lugging buckets of water from a stream, Jak apologized and moved back onto the path.

But then he lost sight of Tamisin. When he finally spotted her again, she was walking next to a tall, thin boy heading toward a large group of fairies. They stopped at a table where other fairies were gathered. The boy turned his head and Jak saw that his skin was an odd shade of blue and his hair was blue black.

It wasn't long before Tamisin and the blue boy reached a spot where green-haired nymphs served food and drinks on a large flat rock covered with a filmy cloth. Fairies of all sizes were clustered around the rock, nibbling fruit and talking. A short distance away, fairy warriors were preparing for battle, but the main topic of conversation of the other fairies of Oberon's court seemed to be the dance that was planned for that night.

Jak stayed back as Tamisin helped herself to a delicate tulip cup filled with some kind of liquid and selected a piece of fruit from a leaf platter. He watched as the blue boy frowned and said something to Tamisin when she reached for another piece. Her hand hovered over the fruit as if she really wanted it, but she looked up at the boy, then took her hand away. Jak heard a strange low sound and realized that it was coming from his own throat. He was growling. That blue boy was telling Tamisin what to do, and Jak didn't like it.

Tamisin and the blue boy strolled off, leaving Jak on the far side of the group of fairies. He was looking for a way to go around them without being conspicuous when a trio of fairies spied him. Jak tried to ignore them as they pointed at him and giggled, talking about him in loud whispers, but when the orange-haired fairy approached him with the others right behind, he had to stop or risk making a scene.

"You're new here, aren't you?" the orange-haired fairy asked. Her gown was orange, too, and she would have been hard to miss in any crowd. When she stopped, a second fairy came to stand beside her. Her bright yellow gown seemed to give off a light of its own, and she had a wide face with large dark eyes that studied him as if he were some sort of slime mold. The third member of their group was a male fairy dressed in greens and browns. He nodded stiffly when Jak glanced his way, then turned aside as if bored.

"Yes, I just arrived," Jak told the orange-haired fairy.

"I'm Lily," she said, giving him a sultry look, "and these are my friends Sunflower and Hawthorne. And you are . . ."

"Nihlo," he said, sticking with the name he'd already given. He started to edge around them, hoping they could take a hint, but Lily stepped in front of him. "I really need to go," he told her. "If you'll excuse me . . ."

"What kind of being are you?" Lily asked.

Jak hesitated. The fairy was forthright to the point of being rude, but maybe that was common in Oberon's court. "I'm a cat goblin and—" Jak began.

"Cat goblin! Lily just loves cat goblins!" Sunflower said, and laughed so loud that all the fairies standing nearby turned to look.

Jak peered past the assembled fairies, looking for Tamisin, but she was no longer in sight.

"If you need someone to show you around, I'm available," said Lily.

Hawthorne looked at her as if she'd lost her mind.

A jostling, thumping sound made everyone turn to look at the two warrior fairies sprinting past, carrying baskets filled with reeds. These were bigger reeds than the kind Lieutenant Spruce and his fairies had carried, and Jak recognized them, having seen them used in battle. When Titania's fairies had fought his uncle Targin's goblins, they had filled such reeds with dust of various colors. If Jak was to find pink dust, his best bet might be to follow these fairies.

"Good day," Jak said, and this time he sidestepped Lily and her friends before they could get in his way.

Jak didn't want it to be too obvious that he was following the warriors, so he walked slowly until he was out of sight of the gathered fairies before he began to hurry. When something boomed and voices cried out, the warriors began to run. Jak ran, too, abandoning the path to cut across the forest. He slowed as the fairies entered a clearing and set their baskets on the ground beside fairies who were already there. The new arrivals were talking to the other warriors when Jak crept through the trees to a sheltering maple, where he hoped to see what was going on.

As soon as he saw what they were doing, Jak knew he had come to the right place. The fairies who had brought the reeds handed them off to other warriors who were waiting. While the runners left the clearing, the new warriors took reeds from the baskets, filled them with dust from some round, squat jugs, and handed them to other runners, who carried the filled reeds to the far end of the meadow.

Unable to see the color of the dust, Jak climbed a tree to get a better look and almost fell out when he saw the number of warriors preparing for battle. He knew that Oberon had an army, but he'd never really thought about what that meant. The sky was alive with tiny fairies taking off and landing.

Hearing voices below him, Jak turned back to the warriors filling reeds and saw that more runners had arrived bringing more jugs of dust. From his new vantage point, Jak was pleased to see that he had a better view of the dust. The first few jugs were filled with yellow, the next held purple, the one after that held green, and, down at the end where he couldn't quite see . . . blue.

Jak didn't know what to do now. None of the jugs held pink dust. But if it wasn't here, where was he going to find it? Perhaps the sphinxes had been mistaken. Perhaps it wasn't pink dust he needed, but one of the other colors. If that were true, however, how would he know which one?

A whisper of sound made Jak start to turn around, and then he felt a hand on his ankle and his heart skipped a beat. He looked down, expecting to see one of Oberon's warriors, but it was Lily, the orange-haired fairy.

"Shh!" she whispered with her finger to her lips. "You

have a choice. You can go with me and answer my questions, or I can start yelling and let all these brave, strong warriors know that they have a spy in their midst. Which one is it going to be?"

"I'll be right there," Jak replied.

Fearing that Lily would go back on her word and sound the alarm anyway, he scarcely breathed as he climbed out of the tree and followed her through the forest. When they were well away from the meadow, Lily stopped and sat down on the trunk of a fallen tree. Patting the trunk beside her, she said, "Sit," and waited for Jak.

"I wasn't spying," Jak told her, although in a way he knew he was. He was also sure that no one would believe him if he told the truth, which he wasn't about to try, because it was their king's magic that he wanted to undo.

"Yeah, right," Lily said, and pointed at the trunk beside her.

Jak sat as far from her as he could. "Let me guess: you want to know why I was in that tree."

Lily laughed and shook her head. "Not at all. I want you to tell me about Tamisin."

"What makes you think I know anything about her?" Jak asked.

"I saw the way you were watching her. You know her from somewhere, don't you? You came here because of her. Tell me the truth or I'll start screaming, and then I'll tell the warriors that you were spying on them."

"Yes, I know her," Jak said reluctantly.

"Where did you meet her?"

"At school," said Jak.

"Do you mean that horrible goblin school on that dreadful island out in the middle of nowhere? I've heard about that place. It sounds like torture to me. What happened? Was she making the royal rounds and stopped there to brighten the day of the poor little goblins trapped on the island? I bet honey wouldn't dissolve in her mouth, that goody-two wings!"

"She's not like that," Jak said, even though he'd resolved not to tell Lily anything.

Obviously agitated, Lily hopped off the trunk and began to pace. "Don't defend her to me!" she said, waving her hands in the air. "I've seen the way she smiles at everyone and acts like she's their friend. Well, I don't believe it for a minute! No fairy is that nice. She's up to something, and I want to know what it is!"

"Tamisin isn't up to anything!" Jak said, getting to his feet. "She's a good person with a kind heart, and I don't want to hear you talk about her like that!"

"Aha! The truth is out!" Lily cried, clapping her hands. "You're in love with her. That's why you came to court! Just wait until I tell everyone that a goblin is madly in love with our *beautiful* princess and she doesn't love him, so he ... Wait, could I be wrong? She does love you, doesn't she?" Lily asked, seeing Jak's expression. "That's even better! Tamisin has a secret that she doesn't want anyone to know! I think at this moment that I love you myself, just a little bit. Come here and I'll give you a kiss."

"No, thanks," said Jak, turning his face away.

"You're saving yourself for her, aren't you? Well, we'll see about that. Tonight at the dance you'll dance with me. Everyone will be there, including your precious Tamisin. I can't wait to see the look on her face when you choose me as your partner. And you will choose me, or I'll tell everyone that you're a spy. Understand, goblin?"

Jak nodded, feeling miserable. He was certain that Tamisin probably wouldn't even remember him or care if he danced with every fairy girl there. When he turned to Lily again, she was doing a little happy dance; Jak couldn't bear to talk to her any longer. There had to be some way to get her to leave him alone, even if it was just for a while. "If there's a dance tonight, shouldn't you be getting ready?" he asked. "The sun is already going down."

Lily laughed and shook her head. "I don't need to get ready. I'm always dressed for a dance!"

"Really?" said Jak. "Because you might want to take a brush to your hair and powder your nose or whatever girls do before a dance. I like your freckles, by the way."

"Freckles!" shrieked Lily. "I don't have freckles! Let me see . . ." Reaching into a fold in her dress, the fairy pulled out a small wooden box shaped like a lily blossom. She pressed a latch on the side and the top sprang open, revealing a rabbit-tail powder puff.

Jak was about to slip away when he noticed that the powder wasn't powder at all, but bright pink fairy dust that covered the fairy's freckles and faded to the color of her skin. It was the very dust he needed. Now all he had to do was get it from her.

"Let me see," Jak said as he approached the fairy girl. Taking the box from her hand, he swiped the rabbit's foot in the dust, then patted it on Lily's nose. "That's much better," he said, and tucked the box in his pocket. "I'll see you at the dance."

Jak was already walking away when Lily called out, "Aren't you forgetting something?" He turned around to see that the fairy was holding out her hand. "My powder?"

Pulling the wooden box from his pocket, Jak strode back and handed it to her. She tucked it in the fold in her dress and said, "The first dance is mine."

Jak was smiling as he walked away. Sticking his hand in his pocket, he rubbed the pink fairy dust between his fingers and laughed. Now all he had to do was find Tamisin, and avoid going to that dance.

# Chapter 20

Jak had hoped to find Tamisin before the dance, but once the sun went down, he realized that he didn't know his way around Oberon's forest and was in danger of getting lost. He asked a passing nymph where the dance was going to be held and followed her directions to a large meadow between a stream and a wall of briars. The edge of the meadow was already crowded with milling fairies; a table made of split tree trunks had been set up at the far end. When Jak didn't see Tamisin anywhere, he wandered over to the table, hoping to get something to quiet his grumbling stomach.

A woman with a smiling face presided over the table where nymphs were already serving drinks in tulip cups. Jak was surprised when the woman turned around and he saw another smiling face on the back of her head. She gestured to him and handed him a cup and a piece of crunchy brown bread slathered with squashed raspberries. "You're Princess Tamisin's friend, aren't you?" she asked, leaning close so no one else could hear. "Malcolm told me about you."

"Do you know the princess?" Jak asked, his mouth watering at the nutty aroma of the bread.

"Go ahead and eat!" said the woman. "My name is Irinia, by the way. I like your Tamisin. Just about everyone who isn't a fairy does. She's nicer than most fairies. I'm not surprised she has a goblin boyfriend."

Jak swallowed the food in his mouth. "I thought that was supposed to be a secret," he said, searching the crowd for Lily and hoping he wouldn't find her.

"If you mean that unsavory piece of work, Lily, she doesn't know what she's talking about. Everyone knows that you're here because of the princess—everyone who isn't a fairy, that is. We have eyes and ears everywhere, we just don't advertise it. Look, there's your princess. You won't be able to get near her for a while, not with those warriors around her. The fighting must be heating up. I suspect they think Titania will try to take her daughter back now. I hope that doesn't happen. There are always innocent casualties when fairies fight fairies, and with all the fairies around here who don't like Tamisin, an accident is bound to happen regardless of who wins. It would be a lot better for both sides if she just disappeared. With a good friend maybe. One who really cares about her. Tonight."

"Why don't they like Tamisin?"

"Jealousy mostly. Or they don't like her mother. Some think the princess is here to spy on Oberon. They think you might be a spy, too, so leaving as soon as you can would be best for both of you."

Jak smiled at Irinia. "You know a lot about a lot of things, don't you?"

The woman chuckled. "Must be because I can see things coming and going."

"Why are they holding this dance when there's fighting going on?"

Irinia shrugged. "Because they're fairies. They dance every night regardless of what else is happening. Listen, the musicians are tuning up now. The dance will start in a few minutes."

Jak glanced at the little group of beings holding instruments. A satyr was playing pan pipes beside a brownie and gnome, both of whom were tooting flutes. Another gnome sat on a stump on their other side, thumping away on a small, round drum. After a minute or two of discordant notes, the little orchestra began to play bright, cheerful music and the fairies drifted into the center of the meadow.

"I'm over here, Nihlo!" Lily called to Jak as she waved an orange flower in the air.

Jak glanced from her to Tamisin, who was standing between the blue boy and a fairy warrior. Tamisin looked unhappy as the blue boy gestured toward the meadow.

"He's trying to make her dance," Jak said to himself.

"Well, of course he is," said Irinia. "It is a *dance*, after all."

"Yes, but she shouldn't dance. Not here, not now. There's a full moon tonight. Her dancing will draw Titania's warriors. Excuse me!" Jak said as he started toward the meadow.

Lily latched on to his arm, smirking as she strode beside him through the fairy throng. The music changed, becoming faster and more frenzied. Apparently the blue boy had had enough of Tamisin's protests, because he shook his head, grabbed her hand, and hauled her across the grass. Tamisin looked around, a frantic expression on her face. *She may have forgotten me*, thought Jak, *but she knows what's about to happen.*

Jak glanced at Lily, who was still holding on to his arm as she chattered away, waving to everyone she knew. She seemed to enjoy the shocked looks on the other fairies' faces, clinging to Jak's arm more tightly when she saw them staring. He tried to hurry to Tamisin's side before she began dancing, but Lily finally noticed and pulled back on his arm.

"Oh no, you don't," she said, giving him a sharp pinch with her fingers. "You're dancing with me!" Jak realized it was too late; they were in the midst of all the fairies, who carried them along in a swirling, dipping romp of a dance.

Jak watched as Tamisin, too, was dragged into the crowd. He hoped that the dance and the music were enough to keep her from the steps she always did on the night of a full moon, but when her feet faltered and began to move to their own tempo, he knew that she was helpless to stop herself.

At first the fairies around her laughed when they saw that the princess was out of step. The blue boy tried to force her back into the rhythm, but gave up and stepped aside when she escaped from his grip, twirling across the grass as fairies moved out of her way. Then the laughter stopped and the space around her grew as the fairies realized that something special was happening. This was no ordinary dance. This was the dance that showed what it meant to be a fairy, exulting in their grace, fluidity, and freedom in a way no other dance could. It was as if Tamisin had gone beyond what ordinary fairies could do, and tapped into the purity of what a fairy could be. The dance showed them a vision of what no fairy had seen for many long-lived generations— since before the wall that separated the worlds existed; fairy and human blood mixed could produce something far greater than either one alone.

The music faded as the musicians saw what was happening, and the fairies of Oberon's court stood entranced as Tamisin danced, her mind far away in a place they couldn't reach. Jak was surprised when he noticed that tears of joy trickled down more than one fairy cheek.

And then the fluttering beat of thousands of fairy wings filled the meadow as Titania's warriors arrived. Tamisin was still dancing when the fighting began. Fairies cried out as swarms of hornets and bees shot from the newcomers' reeds. Green dust wafted across the meadow, making the grass grow with amazing speed, tripping some of the dancers and trapping others. Pulling free of Lily's clinging grasp, Jak ran after Tamisin, wrapping his arms around her so that she had to stop dancing. She struggled for a moment, but then her eyes focused on his face and she grew still.

"What are you doing?" she asked.

"Saving you," said Jak even as he swung her off her feet and carried her from the meadow.

Fighting raged around them as Jak struggled to break free, darting past combatants as he tried to avoid the magic that they were using on each other. This was nothing like the battle between the goblins and the fairies that he had witnessed before. This was more vicious as fairy fought fairy, using every tool they had. Warriors tossed sparkling bubbles that exploded on contact, sending fairies flying backward through the air. Reeds shot dust of red or black, making the air burn or become a thick barricade. Ice spread across the ground when one fairy tried to freeze another. Vines wrapped around bodies and throats at another fairy's gesture. Two warriors cast statue spells at each other; they were both turned to stone. More dust wafted through the air when fairy warriors aimed their reeds, and it was all Jak could do to avoid being turned into a slug or growing feet longer than his legs.

"This way!" the brownie who had helped him shouted, pointing in the direction of Irinia and an ogress. Holding Tamisin close to protect her, Jak dashed across the grass to join them as they ran away from the fighting.

At first Jak made no attempt to be quiet; getting away from the fairies was all he could think about. After splashing across the stream, he followed the women and the brownie through the forest. Jak wasn't happy about putting his trust in people he didn't know, and he almost turned back when they entered the meadow where the warriors had been loading their weapons. The meadow was empty, however, so he didn't question them as they continued on through thickly growing trees to a clearing at the base of a rocky outcrop.

"Are you all right?" Jak asked Tamisin as he set her on her feet.

"I'm fine," she said, brushing her hair from her eyes.

Although her hair was in disarray, and her clothes were rumpled, Jak thought she had never looked more beautiful. He paused for a moment just to gaze at her, but when she looked puzzled, he remembered what he needed to do. "Just a minute," he said, and reached into his pocket. Taking out a large pinch of pink fairy dust, he sprinkled it on her and said,

> *Undo the spell*
> *That someone used*
> *To change her worldly view.*
> *Allow her now*
> *To clear her sight*
> *And see that which is true.*

When he finished, he watched her closely, expecting a dramatic change, but nothing seemed to be happening.

"We have to go," said the brownie. "I'm sure they're already looking for her."

Irinia nodded. "Malcolm is right. We need to climb over these rocks to the other side. Narlayna has a boat that you can use to get far away from here."

"I know where the boat is," said Tamisin. "I was there when your father left it for you, Narlayna. Are you sure you won't need it yourself someday?"

"I'm sure," the ogress replied. "You helped me when I was in trouble. Now it's my turn to help you."

Tamisin rubbed her forehead. "My head feels funny. I can't seem to . . ." She glanced up at Jak, her eyes growing wide. "I remember you now! Your face . . . I kept trying to see it . . . Oh, Jak, what did they do to me? How could they make me forget you?"

Jak staggered when she threw her arms around him, but then he was holding her and he couldn't stop smiling. Maybe everything would be all right now. Maybe she'd forget how angry she'd been with him and things would go back to the way they'd been before.

"It was nectar, I bet," said Irinia. "Oberon is known to have a way with nectars."

"He isn't my father, is he?" said Tamisin, lifting her head to look into Jak's eyes. "He had me convinced that Titania was lying, only she wasn't."

"The worst fight they had before this was over Dasras, and neither Titania nor Oberon could claim him as a blood relation," said Irinia. "This fight is already so much nastier than that. Oberon has wanted to be a father for years, so hearing he had a daughter that his wife hadn't told him about was bound to stir up trouble."

Malcolm nodded. "And nothing he could do would make Titania angrier than kidnapping her daughter."

"Who is Dasras?" asked Jak.

"That blue boy I was with," said Tamisin.

"Well, it's over now," said Jak. "And I want to get you out of here."

Tamisin pulled away from him, and Jak knew right away that she'd remembered how things had been between them in the human world. For a moment it looked as if she wanted to say something to him, but then she changed her mind and turned to her other friends. "I have to tell Oberon that he's wrong about me. Maybe then he won't want to fight Titania."

Malcolm snorted. "He wouldn't believe you."

"Maybe not," said Tamisin, "but I have to try. Do any of you know where I can find him?"

"He's probably with his officers, telling them what to do," said Malcolm. "They could be anywhere now."

"Why don't you ask him?" Irinia said, pointing behind her. "Dasras has been watching us from those trees ever since we got here."

# Chapter 21

Tamisin couldn't see anyone among the trees, but Jak began to growl as soon as he glanced in that direction. With one bound, he reached the trees and knocked a shadowy figure to the ground. "What are you doing here?" he snarled.

"I followed you from the dance to make sure you weren't going to hurt the princess," Dasras told him.

"We weren't hurting her; we were rescuing her," Jak said. "If you had a little more backbone, you would have tried to help her yourself."

Tamisin hurried to Jak's side and set her hand on his shoulder. "You can let him up now. There's something I want to ask him."

Jak stepped back and watched with narrowed eyes as the blue boy got to his feet.

"Are you leaving with him?" Dasras asked Tamisin as he moved farther from Jak. "What about me? Don't you love me even a little? Don't you want to stay with me?"

Tamisin's cheeks turned pink. Obviously this boy really hadn't listened to her. "I told you before that I don't love you. I thought I did, maybe a tiny bit, but I didn't, not really. You did something to make me think I loved you, didn't you?"

Dasras looked away as if he could no longer meet her eyes. "I don't know what you're talking about."

"Yes, you do," said Malcolm. "You've been Oberon's little helper for years. You have to know all about the nectar he uses to change people's minds. What did you do, steal some from him?"

"I never stole anything from Oberon," Dasras said, glaring at the brownie.

"But you did use nectar on Tamisin, didn't you?" asked Jak.

"*I* didn't," Dasras said.

Irinia took a step closer and peered into his eyes. "Maybe you didn't, but someone did. Were you there when Oberon used it?"

Dasras shrugged. "It seemed like a good idea at the time, but I guess I didn't move fast enough. If I had, she might really have loved me."

"What do you mean?" asked Tamisin.

Dasras still couldn't look at her. "I waited until he'd used the nectar. After he left, I might have made a small suggestion of my own."

"What did you tell her?" growled Jak.

Dasras's face turned a darker shade of blue. "Nothing really."

"Tell me or I'll make you tell me," Jak threatened, raising his fist.

"And I'll help him," said Narlayna.

"There's no need for that," Dasras hurried to say. "I might have said something about being Tamisin's one true love."

"And?" said Irinia.

Dasras shrugged. "She'd been nattering on about her friend Jak. I could tell from the way she talked about him that he was more than just a friend, so I told her to forget him. That's all," he said, casting a worried look at Narlayna. "I left right after that."

"I don't get it," said Jak. "Why would you tell someone you just met that she was your one true love?"

"I think I know," said Tamisin. "If the daughter of the fairy king loved him, Dasras's place in Oberon's court would be secure. He was worried that Oberon might get tired of having him around one day."

"That's really pitiful," Jak said, shaking his head.

"Did you hear what Oberon said to me when he used the nectar?" Tamisin asked.

"Not really," said Dasras. "Whatever he said he whispered into your ear."

"He must have told you that you were his daughter for you to have believed it so strongly," said Irinia.

Tamisin looked up when there was a loud boom and pink and yellow lights lit the night sky. "We have to hurry. Do you know where Oberon is now?" she asked, turning to Dasras.

"I don't think you should—" Dasras began.

Jak took a step closer to the blue boy. "It doesn't matter what you think. Where is he?"

"In the glade where he meets petitioners," said Dasras.

"He's lying," Irinia told the others. "You can see it in his eyes."

"Dasras, please?" said Tamisin. "I have to talk to him and stop this war. He shouldn't fight over me. I'm not his daughter, and I can prove it to him."

Dasras looked doubtful. "It would have to be good, solid proof."

"It is," Tamisin told him, trying to sound more convinced than she felt.

With Narlayna prodding Dasras from behind and Jak snarling each time he hesitated, the blue boy led them through the forest. They were passing the lake where the sea serpent lived when they ran into a group of full-sized warrior fairies filling reeds with fairy dust. Dozens of fireflies were posted around the small clearing, creating light for the working fairies. When one of the warriors spotted Tamisin and her friends, he stepped forward and held up his hand. "No one is allowed past this point, Your Highness," he said. Then he glanced at Narlayna and Irinia and frowned. "What are you two doing outside the briar hedge? It's way past your curfew."

Tamisin looked around, but Jak and Malcolm had disappeared into the woods. "I asked them to escort me," she said, turning back to the warrior. "I need to speak to Oberon. Would one of you be able to take me to him?"

"I'm sorry, Your Highness, but we have strict orders not to let anyone pass."

"I understand," said Tamisin, "but it's very important that I see him now. I have some information that he needs to hear."

"You could tell me and I'd get a message to him. Other than that . . ."

A loud, chuffing snort came from the lake near where the other fairies were filling the reeds. Suddenly a spout of water shot toward them, drenching the fairies and a basket of already-filled reeds. The fairies shouted, and while some ran around, trying to move the dust-filled jugs, others ran toward the lake where the sea monster was still spraying water in their direction. The warrior who was talking to them looked undecided for a moment, and then he, too, ran off to wave his arms at the sea monster.

"Come on," said Narlayna, hustling Tamisin and Dasras past the fairies and into the trees beyond. Irinia followed a few paces back, watching the fairies with her second set of eyes.

"What happened to Jak and Malcolm?" Tamisin asked once they were out of sight of the fairy warriors.

"I'm right here," grumbled the brownie as he slipped through the trees to join them. "Your friend will be along in a minute. So, his name is Jak, is it? I thought it was supposed to be Nihlo."

"Where did you two go?" asked Tamisin.

Malcolm's mouth twisted in a wry smile. "Someone

had to distract those numbskull fairies. Your friend and I . . . Ah, here he is."

Jak stepped out of the gloom, dripping wet and grinning. "That was the most fun I've had in ages! I thought you were crazy when you said we should use the sea monster," he told Malcolm, "but I'd do it again in a heartbeat. I've never ridden anything that big before. And fast! And the way those fairies ran . . ."

Seeing the joy on Jak's handsome face, Tamisin wondered how she could ever have turned away from him. After treating him so badly, how could she repair the damage she had done? Was it even possible to return to the way things used to be? Feeling embarrassed and guilty, she realized that she didn't have the slightest idea how to apologize to Jak.

"Keep walking," said Narlayna as she gave Dasras a push.

"She's right," Tamisin said, giving herself a mental shake. "We don't have time to waste."

"I didn't think we were wasting time," grumbled Jak even as he followed her through the trees. "Where are we going, anyway?" he asked, poking Dasras with his finger.

"It's not far now," the blue boy said. "We'd be able to see it if it weren't for all these trees."

"Quiet!" whispered Irinia, and they all stopped where they were. A squadron of tiny fairy warriors flew overhead on their way to the lake. None of them seemed to notice Tamisin or her companions, who started walking again once they were gone.

Only a few minutes later, Dasras paused at the base of a tree so big that six men standing fingertip to fingertip couldn't have reached around it. "This is it," he said, and turned to Tamisin. "You're on your own from here."

"I don't see anyone," she said. "Where's Oberon?"

"Up there," said Dasras, pointing into the branches high overhead. "This is the tallest tree in Oberon's forest. I've never been to the top, but I've heard that you can see all the way to Sphinx Alley from there."

"How do we get up there?" Narlayna asked, studying the first branch nearly twenty feet above them. It was so broad that three people could have sat side by side without worrying about falling off.

"You can't, but she can," he said, looking at Tamisin.

"He means I have to fly," she told her friends.

Jak shook his head. "I don't like you going by yourself."

"I'll be back before you know it," Tamisin told him. The look he gave her was filled with such concern and longing that it made her heart skip a beat.

"We'll wait here for you," said Irinia, but Dasras had already disappeared through the trees.

Her friends were arguing about how one of them should climb the tree when Tamisin spread her wings. The wing she had injured the day before was still sore, but she thought it should hold out long enough to carry her to the top of the tree.

"Be careful!" Jak called after her as she beat her wings and rose into the air.

The tree was enormous, rising so high above her that

she began to doubt that her wing could carry her that far. After a time, however, the mighty branches gave way to slimmer versions, and she soon spotted the twinkling lights of fairies. Not sure which one might be Oberon, she called out, "Father! I need to talk to you."

Fairies swirled around Tamisin, then one that was brighter than the rest landed on the branch beside her. A moment later Oberon was full sized and looking tired and worried. "Tamisin, what are you doing here?" he asked. "You shouldn't have come this close to the fighting. You do know that there's a war going on, don't you?"

"That's just it," said Tamisin as she settled on the branch. "This war doesn't need to happen. There's no reason for you to fight with Titania. I know how much you want to think that I'm your daughter, but it just isn't true. Titania wasn't lying when she said that my father was human. I have proof if you don't believe me."

Oberon frowned. "What kind of proof? Surely if your father were human, he'd no longer be alive."

"He's not, but I don't need him to show you that I'm part human. I've had the proof with me all along. Look at my wings. They're larger than a normal fairy's, and I can fly long distances while I'm big. Which is good, because I can't make myself shrink. And look here. My feet are bigger than a normal fairy's." She held one up and waggled it. "I'm not slender like a fairy, and if I ate as little as you do, I'd get sick."

Oberon nodded slowly, glancing from her wings to her feet to her face.

"I tried to find ways that you and I were alike, but there wasn't anything to find!"

"There may be some truth to what you're saying," Oberon told her. From the sound of his voice and the sadness in his eyes, it looked as if such an admission had been hard to make.

"Then please, please stop fighting with Titania! There's no reason for this war to continue!"

"Yes, there is," said Oberon, his expression hardening. "Titania hid your existence from me. I had to learn about you from others, which shamed me in their eyes. It's a matter of honor. She must apologize to me, something I know she will not do. Besides, I cannot stop fighting until she does. I am simply defending my home."

A loud boom shook the air, and the sky lit up in a shower of crimson and purple. Although the colors faded away, Tamisin could still see their images when she closed her eyes. In the brief moment of brilliance, she had seen what Dasras had meant. She wasn't quite at the top of the tree, but she was far above the other trees of the forest and could see for miles, including the northwest corner of the forest where the lights seemed to originate.

Tamisin was gazing off to the far side of the forest when the flurry of fairies returned to swarm around Oberon. He nodded as they drew close. Turning to Tamisin, he said, "I must go. One of my warriors will take you to the glade where we first met. You'll be safe there. We'll talk more on my return."

A moment later Oberon was small again, and then he

was gone, having flown off with the rest of the fairies. Only one fairy remained behind, but when Tamisin said, "You don't need to escort me. I can find my own way," that fairy left as well.

When Tamisin reached the base of the tree, her friends were still there, waiting. "He said that he can't stop fighting until Titania does. And now he's flown off! We'll have to try to see Titania now. I don't want people hurting each other because of me, especially when there's really no reason to fight."

"How do you expect to find her?" asked Malcolm.

"I saw where the lights were coming from," Tamisin told them as she folded her wings and tucked them into the slits in her back. "It's that way."

Narlayna nodded when she saw where Tamisin pointed. "That's the northwest corner," said the ogress. "I passed through there when I came to Oberon's forest. My father's home is on the other side of the river."

"Then you're familiar with the land?" said Jak.

"Somewhat," Narlayna told him.

Tamisin paused as another boom shook the ground and made the tree branches sway overhead. "Then you know it better than the rest of us," she said, looking at the ogress. "You can lead the way."

# Chapter 22

Jak wasn't very good at estimating the size of a piece of land, but from what he'd seen on Lamia Lou's map, Oberon's forest encompassed thousands of acres. It was certainly bigger than the forest where Titania lived, the only other fairy forest that Jak had ever visited. When he sniffed the air, Jak thought Oberon's forest smelled spicier than Titania's, but that might be because of all the fairy dust that the two sides were using on each other. The presence of the dust might also explain why every sound seemed louder than it would have on an ordinary day. When he stepped on a twig and it snapped, Jak's heart began to race.

The farther they walked, the louder the booming grew. Each time they heard it, one or more of Jak's companions would jump. It seemed to bother Irinia the most; every time, she looked startled and let out a soft gasp.

They had reached an older part of the forest that had been left unkempt and natural, where tangled wild roses caught at clothes and fallen tree trunks waited to trip the unwary. Jak could see better than the rest of his companions, so even though Narlayna was supposedly leading the way, Jak steered them past a nasty-looking ravine and around more than one briar patch. He also kept his ears pricked for unusual sounds, which might have been why he heard the tapping before anyone else.

Jak poked Narlayna's shoulder and motioned for her to stop and be silent. She did the same to the others as Jak crept through the trees, following the sound of the light, repetitive tapping.

"Blasted reed is jammed," someone in front of him announced.

"Don't do that! You'll break it!" said a voice that Jak recognized as Ragweed's.

"Then you fix it. I can't get it to . . . Wait. There you go. That should work."

Jak crept close enough to the fairy warriors that he could see them without being seen; it was Ragweed and Mugwort. He watched them inspect their weapons, then shrink and take off into the night sky. When he was sure they were gone, he slipped back to where Tamisin and her friends were waiting.

"Two of Oberon's warriors," he told them in a soft whisper.

"Huh? What's that?" Malcolm grumbled in his normal voice. Irinia nudged him and bent down to whisper in his ear. The brownie nodded and turned his head toward the sky.

"We have to be as quiet as we can," Jak said in a slightly louder voice. "We could run into warriors from either side now."

"Or something worse," said Irinia. "In the last war, both Titania and Oberon drove vicious creatures in front of their armies. I heard two warriors talking about it. They said that it softens up the enemy."

"Do you think they'd do that now, knowing that Tamisin is in these woods?" asked Jak, shooting her a worried glance.

"They would if they thought she was somewhere safe out of the way," said Malcolm.

"They probably both think I'm safe," said Tamisin. "Oberon tried to send me back, remember? And Titania might be mad at Oberon, but I doubt she thinks he would put me in any danger. Even so, I have to keep going. If anyone wants to go back . . ."

When everyone shook their heads, they continued on a little more cautiously than before. They followed a faint animal trail for a time, then left it for the cover of deeper woods when they saw tiny fairies flying overhead. Once they passed through a section of woods that looked as if some sort of blight had taken hold. The leaves of the trees were curled and brown, and dead insects littered the ground. Jak thought the air smelled sour. When he brushed against a branch, it left a smudge of pale blue dust on his sleeve. He didn't tell anyone, but he hurried everyone away from there as quickly as he could.

Not long after that, Tamisin almost tripped over a low

rock wall, but Jak caught her and pulled her back in time. They walked around the wall only to discover that they were in the midst of ruins from long ago, a sign that someone other than fairies had once lived there. Jak would have loved to explore the ruins, and Malcolm seemed just as interested, but no one tried to dawdle as they made their way between rows of stones and out the other side.

A short distance beyond the ruins they came across a creek where moonlight showed them the uneven remains of stone pillars that had once supported an ancient bridge. Jak hesitated at the water's edge, remembering the river at the bottom of the Great Ditch, but Narlayna strode to the bank and stepped off. When she was halfway across, she turned and waved to her friends. "It's waist deep on me and the current is strong. Stay there and I'll carry you across."

A series of loud booms made Irinia and Malcolm cover their ears. When the lights descended only a few hundred feet away, Narlayna turned to slog back through the water. Tamisin and Irinia were standing side by side, so the ogress grabbed them both, tucking one under each of her massive arms. She had just deposited them on the other side when Jak saw a sapling wave wildly behind Tamisin.

"What's that?" he asked Malcolm.

The brownie glanced across the creek, but the movement had already stopped. "I don't see any—"

The sapling broke with a loud crack, and a two-headed troll stumbled out of the underbrush. "Narlayna, go back!" Jak shouted. "Go help Tamisin!"

Another two-headed troll tromped a shrub flat as it joined the first. Branches waved and twigs cracked like gunshots as another troll drew closer. Cupping his hands around his mouth, Malcolm yelled one word: "Trolls!"

Narlayna spun around and lunged toward the shore she had just left. Jak reached into his pocket and pulled out his comb. His eyes darted from the river to the shore, until they fell on the stone pillars. He had already transmogrified the comb into a sword when he leaped onto the first stone column. Wielding the sword in front of him, he jumped from one pillar to the next, finally landing on the far side of the creek.

Another troll had already emerged from the trees, twirling a tree trunk as thick as his upper arm over his three heads. Seeing Tamisin and Irinia, the troll bellowed and ran toward them. Narlayna was already wrestling with one of the other trolls when Jak ran up and swung his sword at the troll carrying the tree trunk.

Jak had learned from his experience with the griffin; this sword was strong, but light. He lunged at the troll. The creature parried the blow easily. However, Jak noticed that when he swung the sword, it created a whistling sound that seemed to bother the troll, making him shake his three heads and scowl. Swinging his sword to make the sound, Jak beat the troll back. And then Malcolm, who had swum across, climbed out of the water and grabbed a sturdy branch. Although the brownie was small, he was strong, and the whack he gave the troll across the knees was hard enough to make the troll howl, drop the tree trunk he was carrying, and bend over.

While Malcolm kept whacking the troll, Jak stepped back and looked for Tamisin. He finally spotted her darting around an ancient, thick-trunked tree while a two-headed troll ran after her, his arms stretched in front of him as he tried to grab her. Irinia was throwing rocks at the troll, but he seemed to be interested only in catching Tamisin.

As Jak drew closer, he could hear the troll talking to himself.

". . . fairy girl!" said one head.

"We eat . . . ," said the other.

". . . her now!"

"Raw!" they shouted in unison.

Jak looked up when two twinkling lights descended from the night sky. They hovered for a moment, and then suddenly Ragweed and Mugwort were there, aiming their reeds at the troll chasing Tamisin.

"Get back, Your Highness!" shouted Mugwort. Raising his reed, he aimed it at the troll and fired a stream of pale purple fairy dust that coated both snarling faces. The troll bellowed with rage and tripped over his toes, which had grown another eight inches.

Mugwort tapped the reed against the palm of his other hand. "This still isn't working right. It was supposed to make his feet grow as long as his arms."

The troll was trying to get up when another boom shook the forest, making everyone stagger.

"Don't worry, Your Highness," said Ragweed. "I'll turn

him to stone with one blast of my . . . Uh, never mind. Something is wrong with this reed, too."

When the fairy dust hit the troll, his skin began to crackle, but instead of turning to stone, it sprouted the soft, yellow down of a duckling. The troll began to scratch his faces and necks with such ferocity that he ripped the down from his skin, leaving angry red furrows.

Jak shook his head. Obviously these fairies weren't going to be much help, but watching Tamisin run around the tree had given him an idea. After turning the sword back into a comb, he tucked it in his pocket and bent down to remove his shoelaces. Picturing a strong, heavy metal cable, he transmogrified first one shoelace, then the other. Leaving one chain on the ground, he hefted the other and called out to Narlayna, "Here! Take the end."

The ogress looked up as Jak swung the end of the cable through the air. Although she looked puzzled, she heaved the troll she'd been fighting to the side, caught the cable with one hand, and watched while Jak used gestures to tell her what to do. It didn't take long for her to understand, and when she did, her lips spread in a wicked grin. Choosing the thickest trunk around, she wrestled the troll in that direction and slammed him against the tree. The troll looked up when Jak and the ogress began to run around him in opposite directions, wrapping him in the cable and securing him to the trunk. With the cable wrapped around him from shoulders to ankles, the troll could do little more than squirm and howl in anguish.

When they were finished securing the troll to the tree,

they turned to the troll that was now fuzzy and yellow. The fairies watched as Jak and Narlayna chained the second troll to the tree behind him, but neither Ragweed nor Mugwort offered to help. They did clap Jak on the back when he was finished, however.

"You know, when I first saw you, I didn't think you were much to look at," said Mugwort, "but you're all right, for a goblin."

"I felt sorry for you," Ragweed told him. "There you were, a common goblin, in love with our princess. I didn't think you stood a chance with her."

"Is that true, Jak?" Tamisin said, brushing her hair from her eyes as she sidestepped the tree holding the troll that had been chasing her. "Did you really tell him that you love me?"

Ragweed answered as if Tamisin were talking to him. "He said it under the influence of truth nectar, so it had to be true."

"Rot and mold!" cursed Malcolm. "That blasted troll got away! I was so busy watching you wrap his friends up that I stopped walloping him for a minute. Wouldn't you know he'd run off when my back was turned?"

"I'll take care of the troll," said Narlayna. "For all we know he might have gone to get more of his friends. At least that's what I'd do if I were him."

"If there are trolls in the woods, we're going to need reinforcements," Ragweed said to Mugwort. "One of us should go with the ogress while the other reports to the colonel."

"I'll go find the colonel," said Mugwort.

"Good, and get us some reeds that work," Ragweed shouted after him as his friend shrank and flew away. He turned around, but Narlayna was already gone. "Hey, wait for me!" he called and took off after her.

Irinia stepped out from the underbrush and glanced at Tamisin. "Was that the same troll who dragged you into his cave? I thought Narlayna had told the fairies about him. They were supposed to send him back to ogre territory."

"The troll did what?" Jak asked, horrified.

"He didn't hurt me," Tamisin reassured him. "Although he did want to eat me. And yes, it was him."

"Then he must have come back with his friends," said Irinia. "I have to say, running into those trolls was the most dreadful thing that has ever happened to me."

"Are you kidding? I haven't had an adventure like this since Oberon brought me here!" Malcolm exclaimed. "I think I'm going to keep this branch and call it my whopping stick," he said, gazing lovingly at the piece of wood he was carrying.

"Did you know it's covered with ants?" asked Irinia.

Malcolm tossed the branch aside and brushed his hands together. "Ugh!" he said. "I can always find another one."

# Chapter 23

Without Narlayna as their guide, Tamisin wasn't sure which way to go. They could go straight ahead, but she thought they had gotten turned around a bit when they walked through the ruins. "I need to see where we are," she said, spreading her wings behind her. "I'm not sure which way to go from here."

"I still don't like the thought of you going anywhere by yourself," Jak said, looking worried.

Tamisin shrugged. "We don't have a choice. I should have reached my mother long before this. Have you noticed that the sound has changed?"

The booming was louder and coming closer together. Unlike the simple spells that had made noses grow and vines twine around ankles, trolls were involved now and there were patches of forest that were dead. The war was changing, and it was only getting worse.

Tamisin's eyes met those of her two friends before she turned to Jak. "If I'm gone longer than ten minutes, Irinia and Malcolm should take you to the beach. I'll meet you there later." It had already occurred to her that if she was going to fly, she might as well fly all the way to her mother. When Jak began to scowl, Tamisin rose into the air before he could try to stop her.

"Wait!" he cried.

"I can't," she called to him. "I should have done this sooner."

Leaving her friends behind was hard, not only because she felt safer when she was with them but because she worried about what might happen to them when they were on their own. Leaving Jak behind was even harder; it felt as if she'd only just found him again.

As she climbed into the night sky, Tamisin began to look around. The higher she flew, the farther she could see, so she rose until the trees lost their individuality and formed a mass below her before she turned northeast. Aside from the fuzzy patches where the dust had spread, the air was clear, with a cool breeze that made her shiver.

Birds flew by now and then, most of them just above the treetops. They seemed to be fleeing from the northeast corner. Tamisin was watching them when she noticed that a loud *thunk* preceded each boom. After the boom, lights arced above the trees, but still not as high as Tamisin was flying. She would have thought the lights exploding below her were pretty if she hadn't known that they were weapons.

Tamisin was eager to see her mother now. She thought of Titania laughing at something she'd said, or looking proud when she saw how well Tamisin could dance on the night all the fairies danced in the moonlit glade. It had meant a lot to her that she was able to do something that made her mother proud. They would never have the relationship that they might have had if Titania hadn't sent her away, but they had begun to create their own special bond. At the thought of the fairy queen fighting for her, Tamisin beat her wings even harder.

When she first started looking for Titania, the night had been silent except for the whisper of her wings and the regular booming. Now Tamisin began to hear a distant rumble; as it grew louder, she realized that it was the sound of falling water. A few minutes later she could see the moonlight reflecting off something shiny. When the next boom sounded, she traced the arc of the lights back to the top of a waterfall. Angling her wings, Tamisin headed in that direction. If her mother wasn't there, she had to be somewhere close by.

As Tamisin began her descent, she finally saw what was making all the noise. In a clearing near the waterfall, fairies were using oversized slingshots to launch large seedpods into the air. When they reached a certain height, the pods exploded, releasing razor-edged seeds that spread out until they hurtled toward the ground in a blaze of light, shredding leaves and cutting through everything below.

Tamisin was wondering how she could reach her mother without flying into the rain of seeds when, out of the corner of her eye, she caught a glimpse of something moving. Turning her head, she saw a shape that had wings but couldn't possibly be a bird. Its body was too long, and it had four legs and a long, thin tail. Tamisin knew when she saw its human face that it was a sphinx. She had never seen one except in mythology books, and even then she hadn't realized just how frightening they could be. As the beast drew closer, Tamisin tried to think of what to do, but her mind was made up for her when the sphinx opened her mouth and roared.

Tamisin dipped her wing, turned, and fled back the way she had come. The wings of the sphinx made a *whump*, *whump* sound that grew louder the closer she flew. "Come back!" the sphinx screamed in a woman's voice, but it was a harsh, ugly noise that made Tamisin beat her wings faster.

Another boom, another shower of lights below her. Tamisin hadn't intended to look back, but when the sphinx screamed again, Tamisin looked without thinking. The sphinx's face was that of an older woman with streaming, gray hair and broken, discolored teeth. Her crazed-looking eyes glared at Tamisin, who abruptly turned away and put everything she had into beating her wings.

She was panting, her lungs aching, when the light of a tiny fairy shot past her. A moment later there were dozens, then hundreds, and the entire sky around her seemed to twinkle. The sphinx roared again as the fairies flew back to surround the beast. Although Tamisin didn't see what the fairies did, the sphinx screamed as if she'd been stuck with pins, turned tail, and flew off.

The wind picked up then, changing from a gentle breeze to a powerful, driving gale. Half the tiny fairies continued to pursue the fleeing sphinx, but the rest turned around and flew to Tamisin, leading her in a spiral down to the ground. Lightning flashed as she landed on a rocky outcrop and felt the first drops of rain.

Tiny fairies joined her. A moment later, one of them grew to human size and Oberon stood beside her. "Look!" he said, holding up his arm to point at clouds gathering in front of the moon. "Titania is using the weather as a weapon."

The storm was getting closer and it was going to be big. Rain and debris whipped through the air. When lightning cracked the night sky, making it as bright as day, Tamisin saw uprooted trees plow through their neighbors, flattening them. Then the hail came, balls of ice bigger than a child's head smashing into the ground with heart-lurching thuds.

Although the rain drenched the ground around Tamisin and Oberon, and the hail hit only feet away, nothing touched either of them. Oberon stood watching the sky as if he expected Titania to tire soon. He didn't seem to notice Tamisin shivering beside him.

The electricity in the air was flowing into her, drawn like metal to a magnet. It crackled along her skin, and when she looked down, she could see it there, a swirling, seething white-gold light caressing her arms and hands. Instead of hurting, it felt warm and invigorating. She let it gather, enjoying the sensation, until her entire body prickled. Although she heard Oberon shouting, the words meant nothing to her. At that moment, the only things that mattered were the storm and the power it was pouring into her.

Even after the wind died down, the clouds broke apart, and the hail stopped entirely, energy continued to fill her. Now it was a burning sensation that seared her nerves with an almost-pain. She would have flung herself out of its reach if she could have, but she was frozen in place, her body rigid.

It didn't occur to Tamisin that she was drawing power from her mother until she dropped her gaze from the sky and found Titania standing in front of her, looking tired and pale. "Are you all right, my darling?" the fairy queen asked, reaching for her daughter.

Tamisin shook her head ever so slightly. Energy crackled off her, making Titania draw back. Concern filled the fairy queen's eyes. "What have you done, Tamisin? What are you doing here with Oberon?"

"I asked him to stop the war," Tamisin said, her voice sounding strange and distant in her own ears, "but he said he was simply defending his home. I was on my way to see you when your storm began. I'm begging you both to stop. This has all been a big misunderstanding. Oberon was certain that I was his daughter. He said that you lied about my father, but I know you didn't. My birth father *was* human, wasn't he?"

Titania sighed. "Yes, my dear, although it would have made things so much easier if he had been fairy."

Tamisin could read the truth in her mother's eyes and knew that only magic could have made her believe that her mother had lied. "There's really no need to fight Oberon," said Tamisin.

"There's more to it than that," said Titania, glancing from Tamisin to Oberon. "Oberon took you by force when you should have been left to live your life as you chose, then lied about me when he should have known that I have never lied to him."

"Is that what you were doing when you didn't contact me or send for me—letting me live my life as I chose?" asked Tamisin, her words catching in her throat.

"Of course, my darling! Did you think I was neglecting you? I kissed you so you would know that I wanted you to visit me, but I never wanted to make you come to the land of the fey unless you wanted to. It was your choice and would have remained so if Oberon hadn't interfered."

"But fighting him like this is wrong! I believe that you still love each other. Mother, Oberon wasn't trying to take me away from you. He just wanted to get to know me."

Sparks shot off Tamisin's fingers and the ends of her hair when she turned to face Oberon. "You used magic to make me stay, but I know that you did it because you wanted to learn more about me. When I thought we were related, I was happy to call you Father. Even though you're not my father, you are married to my mother, which makes you my stepfather. I can still call you Father if you'd like."

A flicker of a smile replaced Oberon's grim expression. "I'd like that," he said, but then he glanced at Titania and the smile vanished. "However, I'm not the one who can stop this war. Talk to the aggressor if you want the fighting to end."

"I came to get back what was mine!" said Titania.

"None of this would have happened if you hadn't sent your fairy to steal Tamisin from her home!"

"And how else was I ever going to meet her? If it had been up to you, I would never have learned of her existence!"

"Please stop!" said Tamisin. She reached for their hands, but stopped when she saw the sparks leaking off her fingers. "I'm asking for one thing, and I've never really asked for anything from either of you before. All I want you to do is *stop fighting* and talk to each other without making accusations. And please agree to this soon, because I feel as if I'm about to explode!"

Titania looked at her, alarmed. The electricity had continued to build inside of Tamisin even after she'd absorbed everything from the storm. She was trying to hold it in, but sparks had started to pour from her fingertips, and she could feel her hair crackling around her. Suddenly Tamisin wasn't sure just how she was going to get rid of it all.

"Yes, yes, of course," said the fairy queen. "What did you do to yourself, Tamisin?"

"I just wanted you to stop fighting," Tamisin said, her voice sounding fainter. It was taking everything she had just to hold in the power.

Titania glanced at Oberon and he nodded. "If Titania has agreed, I no longer have any reason to fight. I'll let it be known that if anyone questions our honor, I'll banish them from all of fairy land. We are the king and queen, after all."

"Thank you," Tamisin whispered, squeezing her eyes shut. "Stand back. I'm not sure how this is going to work."

Although she hoped that they had gotten out of the way, Tamisin was no longer able to look for fear that if she did, the electricity would pour out of her in their direction and burn them to little crisps. Instead she tilted her head back, raised her arms toward the sky, and relaxed, willing the electricity to go straight up.

Like water released from a dam, the power surged through her and out her hands, aiming toward the bare-faced moon. The first rush of electricity tore at her nerves so that her entire being felt scorched and raw, and it was all she could do to stand upright. When the overwhelming excess was gone, the rest flowed through her in a soothing, more controlled way. The deafening roar in her ears made her wonder if she'd ever hear again, but as the last of the electricity trickled out, she heard voices talking, although she couldn't tell what they were saying.

Emptied, Tamisin staggered, but Titania and Oberon were there to hold her up. "Are you all right?" the fairy queen asked.

"I'm better than all right," Tamisin said, and she knew that it was true.

The next morning, Jak and Tamisin were taking their breakfast to the rocks above the shoreline when they saw Titania and Oberon talking to a group of fairies. As Tamisin drew near, Titania moved away from the others to join her.

"I just wanted to tell you that Oberon and I were talking last night, and we may try something we haven't done in a very long time. We're thinking about living together again. Sometimes we would be here, and sometimes in my forest."

Tamisin smiled. "I'm glad to hear that; I bet your fairies will be, too."

"The fairies that I sent to watch over you told me that the gate near your home was closed every time you visited it. We've been having problems with the gates, and now it's time that I looked into it myself. As for returning to the human world—come see me when you're ready to leave. My warriors will escort you to my forest and help you find an open gate. I'm going to stay here for a few days, however. Oberon and I have some catching up to do."

Once they were alone again, Tamisin turned to Jak and said, "I owe you an apology. It wasn't your fault that my mother's kiss made me want to come back, or that the gate wasn't opening and I couldn't get through. I've never been so frustrated in my life! I am sorry I acted kind of crazy, though."

Jak leaned toward her to rest his forehead against hers. "And I'm sorry I didn't help you when you needed me. I didn't know the compulsion Titania placed on you was so strong until you told me that night. I started looking for another gate, but the one behind my house never opened again, and I couldn't find any others that were open. I wanted to tell you, but by then you didn't want to talk to me. Do you believe me when I say that I love you?"

Tamisin laughed. "How could I not believe you? You admitted it under the influence of truth nectar, so it has to be true. The thing is, I love you, too. I may not have shown it, but I never stopped loving you. I was miserable without you. My poor parents couldn't figure out what was wrong with me." Tamisin frowned and her eyes grew distant. "I left without leaving word. My parents have no idea what happened to me. I wonder how much time has passed."

"You'll be back soon, and you can tell your parents what happened. I just hope we haven't missed our entire summer vacation," said Jak.

Tamisin looked horrified. "That would be awful! I had so much planned!"

"I hope those plans include me," Jak told her.

"From now on all my plans are going to include you. And the first thing I plan to do is this." Her eyes were shining when she brushed Jak's lips with a feather-light kiss. Suddenly his arms were around her and the kiss was anything but light.

# Author's Note

William Shakespeare's *A Midsummer Night's Dream* was the inspiration for both *Fairy Wings* and *Fairy Lies*. Titania, Bottom, Oberon, and the young orphan boy (whom I named Dasras) were all characters in the play.

# DON'T MISS AN ALL-NEW FAIRY TALE FROM E. D. BAKER!

Serafina is living the normal life of a village girl when she gets a mysterious letter from a great-aunt she's never heard of. Little does Fina know, her great-aunt has some magical abilities and lives in an even more magical cottage...

**READ ON FOR A SNEAK PEEK OF A QUESTION OF MAGIC.**

Serafina watched as Alek folded the metal back on itself and used a heavy mallet to beat it flat once again. He was making a sword for Sir Ganya, a local knight who had promised more work if this piece turned out well. Serafina always enjoyed watching Alek, whether he was making horseshoes, nails, or something as refined as a sword. Although his father specialized in plows and axles and things ordinary people needed, Alek preferred to work on things that required a more precise touch.

Alek's father, Kovar, grinned at Serafina from the other side of the blacksmith shop. Everyone knew that Serafina liked seeing how things were done. Her own father's nickname for her was Kitten because he swore that she was as curious as a cat. Whether she was watching someone work or asking questions about things she didn't understand, Serafina was always interested in learning something new.

"When you finish working on that sword for the day, you can help me take off the axle I'm fixing next," Alek's father told him. "The farmer who brought the wagon in wants it as soon as possible."

Alek nodded and wiped the sweat from his eyes. His father was a strong man, but Serafina had seen Alek lift almost as much weight.

"Miss Serafina! There you are!" Tasya, her mother's servant girl, waved at her from the doorway. "A letter came for you! Your mother wants you to come home now. Everyone is waiting for you to read it!"

Serafina's eyes went wide. A letter was always a big event, and she could imagine how excited her family must be. "I'll come back to tell you what it is as soon as I can," she told Alek.

He had been her best friend since they were children, but in the last few years he'd become something more. After her family, he would be the next person to hear any news she had to share.

\* \* \*

Serafina was reaching for the door to her parents' house when it flew open and her sister stepped out. "There you are!" snapped Alina. "We've been waiting for you to come home."

"How are you?" Serafina asked her.

Alina rubbed her belly. "I think the baby will be here soon. I've been having little pains for the last few days. And look at my ankles!" she said, lifting the hem of her skirt. "They're so swollen I can't lace up my boots. Come into the kitchen. I need to sit down. Nesha Zloto is here," she added in a whisper. "The old gossip is in the kitchen with Mother and won't leave until you read the letter."

Serafina's father, the most sought-after master builder in the town of Kamien Dom in the kingdom of Pazurskie, had encouraged his youngest daughter to learn to read and write. No one else in her family had been interested. After Serafina learned, she taught Alek and often shared her books with him.

Someone laughed inside the kitchen as Serafina followed Alina through the door. Their mother, Zita, was seated at the table across from an older, white-haired woman. Tasya had gone into the kitchen before the girls and was already pouring hot water into the teapot.

Zita's eyes lit up in a way that always made Serafina feel warm inside.

"Oh, good, you're here, Fina!" said Zita. "Tasya, I'll take care of the tea. I want you to run over to Katya's house and tell her that Fina is back."

Tasya set the pot on the table, wiped her hands on her apron, and hurried from the kitchen. Alina took a seat beside her mother's chair and sighed.

Their neighbor, Widow Zloto, scowled when she glanced at the girls. "Alina can sit at the corner like that; just make sure you don't, Serafina. Move over! Alina is already married, so it won't affect her, but unmarried girls who sit at a corner will stay single for seven more years."

"Good day, Mistress Zloto," Serafina said, bending down to kiss the old woman's wrinkled cheek.

The Widow Zloto patted Serafina's hand. "You can fetch me some of that good bread your mother makes, Fina."

"I'll have some, too," said Alina.

"I'll bring a plate to share," Serafina told them. She had already spotted the letter on the table, propped against a mug filled with daisies. Her fingers itched to pick up the letter, but instead she hurried to get the bread and cheese.

The bread was the traditional round loaf topped with salt usually given to guests and special company.

Her mother made one every day, knowing that at least one of the neighbors was bound to stop by.

"Don't forget the knife!" cried Widow Zloto. "It's bad luck to break bread with your hands. Break a loaf, break a life; that's what my mother used to say."

Serafina smiled. The old woman was one of the most superstitious people she knew, and she mentioned the knife every time she ate a piece of bread.

Alina leaned forward to rub the small of her back. "Hurry, Serafina! I want to hear your letter before this baby is born!"

"Your baby isn't coming this very minute," Widow Zloto told her. "But when it comes, you make sure no stranger sees it until it's at least two months old. It's bad luck if they do!" The sisters called out along with the old woman, then laughed when she laughed, too. "So, I'm a little superstitious? What can I say, my mother was just as bad and my grandmother was even worse. But your sister is right, Serafina. Hurry so we can hear what's in the letter. I wonder who sent it."

Serafina couldn't imagine who might have written to her. Aside from her father, people in her family rarely received letters. When they did, everyone wanted to be there for the first reading. Because she and her father were the only ones in the family who knew how to read, they were often asked to read the letters over and over again. The few letters they did receive were usually their only connection with some of their friends and relatives and were generally treasured and set aside to keep.

Serafina's mind raced as she tried to think of who might have sent *her* a letter. Could it be one of her cousins inviting her to visit? Perhaps it was her old friend Eva whose family had moved away the year before. Serafina was pondering the possibilities as she carried the still-warm bread to the table.

The door opened as her oldest sister, Katya, burst into the kitchen, out of breath from running. "Oh, good! I'm not too late!" she said, collapsing into a chair. "Mother, the children were taking their naps, so I asked Tasya to stay and watch them. I hope you don't mind."

"Not at all," said Zita.

"It's good that Tasya won't be here," declared Widow Zloto. "Servants love to gossip. Whatever your letter says would be all over town before nightfall. I know— you should hear what my serving girl tells me!"

"You sit down now, Fina," said her mother. "Read the letter while I take care of the food. We can't stand the suspense any longer."

Serafina set the knife on the table, slid into her seat, reached for the letter, and turned it over in her hands.

She had hoped to see who had sent it, but the writing on the back simply said "Serafina Divis."

"What does it say?" Alina asked, leaning toward the table.

"Just my name," said Serafina. "No address or anything."

Even the stamp used to press the sealing wax had been plain, without the usual initial or decoration. Frowning in concentration, Serafina broke the wax and spread the letter open on the table.

"Don't start yet, Fina!" said Katya. "Let Mother sit down and get comfortable. I'm just sorry Father is away," she added. "He would love to hear the letter, I'm sure. All right. You can start now."

Serafina glanced from one person to the next. "Are you certain I can read it? No one has to fetch someone else or start supper or—"

"Just read the thing!" Alina ordered, kicking her leg under the table.

Serafina grinned, but her hands were shaking when she began.

*Dear Serafina,*
  *I am sure you have never heard of me,*
*but I am your great-aunt Sylanna from*

*your grandmother Yanamaria's side. I am*
*writing to inform you of the inheritance*
*that I intend to leave you. This*
*inheritance is of great importance and*
*will change your life forever. Should you be*
*interested in this bequest, come to the*
*town of Mala Kapusta on the next market*
*day. At nine o'clock that night, go to the*
*house located at the western-most edge of*
*the town, past the Bialy Jelen tavern.*

*Looking forward to your arrival,*
*Your great-aunt Sylanna*

"She's right. I've never heard of her," said Alina. "Who is Sylanna? And why is she leaving anything to Fina? Why not me or Katya? We're older, after all. Mother, have you ever heard of this person?"

"The name isn't familiar, but then your grandmother had so many sisters. Some of them died young, others moved away."

"An inheritance!" said Widow Zloto. "Well, well! We might have a little heiress here! I do wonder why she chose you for this honor? Not that you aren't deserving, dear child, but your sisters have been completely cut out."

"It isn't fair!" complained Alina.

"I'm sure Great-Aunt Sylanna had a reason," said Katya. "But I can't imagine why she would pass over two older sisters for Fina."

"What do you suppose it is?" their mother mused.

"Money, of course," said Widow Zloto. "Inheriting a lot of money would change anyone's life."

"Perhaps it's a small business," said Katya. "Then she'd have to move to Mala Kapusta. It makes sense that she'd inherit that. Both Alina and I have families of our own and can't just pick up and leave."

"We won't know why I was named or what my inheritance is until I go to claim it," Serafina declared. "Do you think Father will be home in time to take me?"

Her mother shook her head. "He'll be gone for another week at least. The next market day is tomorrow."

"I wish Alek could go with me—but I know it wouldn't be proper, so I won't ask him," she hurried to say, even as her mother and Widow Zloto opened their mouths to protest. Serafina turned to Alina, but she knew the answer even before she asked. "I don't suppose that Yevhen—"

"He can't go anywhere! How can you ask with the baby coming so soon?"

"I know, I know. Plus he's busy taking inventory in

his father's warehouse," said Serafina. Alina's husband worked for his father, a successful wine merchant.

"Why doesn't Viktor take her?" asked Widow Zloto. "He's always so busy, but he can take a day off for that, surely?"

As one of her father's apprentices, Viktor had lived with the family for seven years and then another two as a journeyman. Soon after receiving his master builder's certificate, he'd married Katya and they'd moved into their own small home.

Serafina was just a little girl when Viktor had started his apprenticeship. On his first day there, she had caught him rifling through another apprentice's belongings. He was so good at lying, however, that no one believed her. After that, Viktor had shown that he didn't like her in lots of little ways, making fun of her when her parents weren't around, pulling her hair when no one was looking. Her favorite necklace went missing one day and turned up broken the next. Serafina was certain that Viktor had done it. Things hadn't gotten much better between them since.

"Of course Viktor can go," said Katya.

"But—" began Serafina.

"Then it's settled," said her mother. "You'll leave early in the morning and be there by supper time. I'm sure

Great-Aunt Sylanna will invite you to spend the night, and you can return the next day."

From the look in her mother's eye, Serafina knew there wasn't any point in arguing. She sat back as the women began to talk of other things, wondering how she was going to stand spending so much time with Viktor.

# E. D. BAKER

made her international debut with *The Frog Princess*, which was a Texas Lone Star Reading List Book, a Book Sense Children's Pick, a Florida's Sunshine State Young Readers List book, and the inspiration for the hit Disney movie *The Princess and the Frog*.

Ms. Baker has written eight books in the Tales of the Frog Princess series, as well as *The Wide-Awake Princess*, *Unlocking the Spell*, and *Fairy Wings*. She lives on a small farm in Maryland, where she and her family breed horses. They also have dogs, cats, goats, and two ducks named Quackers and Fromage.

www.talesofedbaker.com

Read all the books in the
Tales of the Frog Princess series!

"[A] brilliantly created world of magic and mayhem." —*VOYA*

www.talesofedbaker.com

# Sleeping Beauty's sister is very much awake . . .

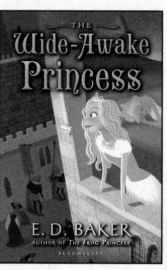

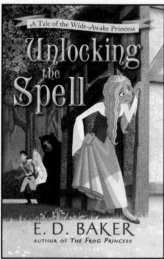